Acc

The Very

"M. Christian speaks with a totally unique and truly fascinating voice. There are a lot of writers out there who'd better protect their markets—M. Christian has arrived!"

—Mike Resnick, Hugo and Nebula
Award-Winning Author

"M. Christian is a hybrid artist and knockout stylist on the order of Jonathan Lethem. Hard-boiled, sharp-edged, funny, and fierce."

—Jim Gladstone, Author,
The Big Book of Misunderstanding

"Combines queer and supernatural/horror fiction, with touches of erotica. Vampire protagonist Valentino is a reluctant trainee in the supernatural international law enforcement organization, *Le Counseil Carmin.* He half-heartedly assists his mentor, Pogue, in enforcing the rules in San Francisco—that is, until Pogue goes missing and Valentino must strive to rise to the occasion to rid the City by the Bay of trouble in the form of the Very Bloody Marys and a deadly faery or two, using what he recalls of his training and the limited resources at his disposal. Readers will never view night life in San Francisco quite the same way. A welcome addition to the vampire noir genre."

—Maryelizabeth Hart,
Mysterious Galaxy, San Diego

"Interesting and modern characters, a bit of local San Francisco color, and a clever mystery twist."

—Brian Youmans, Editor,
Suddenly Press

NOTES FOR PROFESSIONAL LIBRARIANS AND LIBRARY USERS

This is an original book title published by The Haworth Positronic Press™, Harrington Park Press®, the trade division of The Haworth Press, Inc. Unless otherwise noted in specific chapters with attribution, materials in this book have not been previously published elsewhere in any format or language.

CONSERVATION AND PRESERVATION NOTES

All books published by The Haworth Press, Inc. and its imprints are printed on certified pH neutral, acid-free book grade paper. This paper meets the minimum requirements of American National Standard for Information Sciences-Permanence of Paper for Printed Material, ANSI Z39.48-1984.

DIGITAL OBJECT IDENTIFIER (DOI) LINKING

The Haworth Press is participating in reference linking for elements of our original books. (For more information on reference linking initiatives, please consult the CrossRef Web site at www.crossref.org.) When citing an element of this book such as a chapter, include the element's Digital Object Identifier (DOI) as the last item of the reference. A Digital Object Identifier is a persistent, authoritative, and unique identifier that a publisher assigns to each element of a book. Because of its persistence, DOIs will enable The Haworth Press and other publishers to link to the element referenced, and the link will not break over time. This will be a great resource in scholarly research.

The Very Bloody Marys

THE HAWORTH POSITRONIC PRESS™
Harrington Park Press®
Greg Herren
Editor in Chief

Mahu by Neil S. Plakcy

Echelon's End: PlanetFall by E. Robert Dunn

Slaves of the Empire by Aaron Travis

The Danger Dance by Caro Soles

Vintage: A Ghost Story by Steve Berman

Drop . . . Dead: The DJ Murders by Tonne Serah

The Very Bloody Marys by M. Christian

The Very Bloody Marys

M. Christian

HAWORTH
POSITRONIC
PRESS

The Haworth Positronic Press™
Harrington Park Press®
The Trade Division of The Haworth Press, Inc.
New York • London

For more information on this book or to order, visit
http://www.haworthpress.com/store/product.asp?sku=5329

or call 1-800-HAWORTH (800-429-6784) in the United States and Canada
or (607) 722-5857 outside the United States and Canada

or contact orders@HaworthPress.com

Published by

The Haworth Positronic Press™, Harrington Park Press®, the trade division of The Haworth Press, Inc., 10 Alice Street, Binghamton, NY 13904-1580.

Cover design by Lora Wiggins.

Library of Congress Cataloging-in-Publication Data

Christian, M.
The very bloody Marys / M. Christian.
p. cm.
ISBN: 978-1-56023-535-4 (pbk. : alk. paper)
1. Vampires—Fiction. 2. Gay men—Fiction. 3. Police—Fiction. 4. San Francisco (Calif.)—Fiction. I. Title.

PS3603.H747V37 2007
813'.6—dc22

2006035688

For Jill

The universe is not only queerer than we imagine, but queerer than we can imagine.

—J. B. S. Haldane

Other Works by M. Christian

Novels:
Running Dry
The Very Bloody Marys

Collections:
Dirty Words: Provocative Erotica
Speaking Parts: Provocative Lesbian Erotica
The Bachelor Machine: Erotic Science Fiction

As Editor:
Blood Lust: Gay Vampire Stories (with Todd Gregory)
Amazons (with Sage Vivant)
Confessions (with Sage Vivant)
Garden of Perverse (with Sage Vivant)
Leather, Lace & Lust: Putting it on to Get Off (with Sage Vivant)
Transgender Erotica: Trans Figures
Bisexual Erotica: The Best of Both Worlds (with Sage Vivant)
Best S/M Erotica 2: More Extreme Stories of Extreme Sex
Love Under Foot: An Erotic Celebration of Feet (with Greg Wharton)
Bad Boys: Steamy Stories from Bathhouses, Backroom Bars, and Sex Clubs (with Paul J. Willis)
The Mammoth Book of Tales of the Road (with Maxim Jakubowski)
The Mammoth Book of Future Cops (with Maxim Jakubowski)
Best S/M Erotica: Extreme Stories of Extreme Sex
The Burning Pen: Sex Writers on Sex Writing
Roughed Up: More Tales of Gay Men, Sex and Power (with Simon Sheppard)
Guilty Pleasures: True Tales of Erotic Indulgence
Rough Stuff: Tales of Gay Men, Sex and Power (with Simon Sheppard)
Midsummer Night's Dreams: One Story, Many Tales
Eros Ex Machina: Eroticizing the Mechanical

Prologue

Momma always said I'd never amount to anything. Of course that was two hundred-something years ago, so maybe she was on to something.

The Very Bloody Marys

doi:10.1300/5329_a

I

It was one of those awful San Francisco nights: a heartbreaker wrapped up in a smothering fog smelling like diesel oil leaking from a busted-up truck, the streets all reflective with the tears of a thousand broken hearts, and the bloated bodies of all those leaping lovers floating up from the icy darkness of the bay . . .

Nah, too much of a downer. Besides, Hammett and Chandler—or at least the fifty million trench-coated, alcoholic, chain-smoking Bogarts who worshipped them—would have my balls on an outrageously baroque platter.

This is the city. Half a million people trying to carve out their own piece of the American pie, serve it up on affordable china purchased on credit from a moderately upscale chain store to their 2.5 kids, spicing it up every once in a while with a clumsy fondle of the babysitter or the tennis coach. It's not a bad city, as cities go, full of pretty good, fairly decent people who usually play by the rules. But when they don't that's where I come in. My name is Valentino.

Yeah, like Friday and the rest of his bullnecked cronies on the other side of that thin blue line would let me get away with that. Besides, I don't have a badge. Okay, let's try again.

I reckon it's a common enough thing with most folks that they think they have a pretty darned good understanding of the ways and means of this here Earth we be sittin' on. Ask 'em and they might look down, say, at their boots, and maybe dig up a bit of their fertile, local soil with a leather tip and say in a low, humble-like tone that they don't really know it all, that there should likely be all kinds of mysteries and unknowns and stuff all hidden and secret. But just as soon as they hem and haw out those words their faces done lift up and you can clearly see—plain see, I say—the smiles on their faces, saying more than anything they might speak out loud that they really do know how everything is, the ways and means of it all. But I can tell you, honestly and forthrightly, my friend, that these people—while good in the heart and blessed with a pair of fine seeing eyes, a discerning set of buds in their strong mouths,

The Very Bloody Marys

doi:10.1300/5329_01

carefully listening ears, and all the rest of their attuned-like senses—really, truly haven't the faintest idea what's going on right under those noses, in front of those eyes, and even deep under the rich soil beneath their boots. How do I know that, you may rightfully ask? How is it that I know what these fine members of humanity do not? Well, friend, I know because of one simple fact, a statement that I believe will demonstrate my expertise in such matters of the cryptic and the arcane, the weird and the veiled. See, I may have my own pair of peepers, taste with the best of them, walk the same dusty avenues, listen to the same tune, live or recorded. I have, shall we say, a rightly unusual perspective on such matters, being as I am not at all human.

Well, shucky-darn and slap me silly, clean out my corncob pipe with my trusty pocket knife, and hock tabbacky at that there spittoon; that ain't rightfully it, either.

Okay, face it. Stare the facts right in the face; own up to it: I overslept. Didn't see that one coming, did you? I should have gotten up at the crack of seven—p.m., of course—and gotten right to work. Hit the bricks, pounded the pavement, done my duty, and all that shit, but I didn't. Barbra came on, magnificent Hebe pipes warbling "people who need people" when my battered yet usually beloved clock radio went one minute beyond 6:59—p.m., of course—and instead of rising and shining, getting that worm, yackita, yackita, instead I flailed and floundered until one of my limbs just happened to connect with SNOOZE, and I did just that for at least another hour and a half.

I didn't even have a good excuse to whack away ninety minutes of grade-A prime nighttime. No wild parties, no frantic debaucheries, no late-night film fests featuring obscure German directors, not even a lively trick—not that I would have turned one down, you understand, it being a long time, a very long time, since I'd had that reason to belt SNOOZE right between the SNEW and the OOZE. Nope, hate to say it, but nothing exciting or interesting kept me in bed that night—just wanting more sleep, and really not wanting to get up and go to work.

In the end, though, even my dream-hazed, sleep-addled consciousness couldn't keep me out of the marching band of responsibility. Okay, that, and Barbra had been replaced by unnecessarily and inexplicably thumping rap.

Up, not bright and certainly not early, I scratched, yawned, stretched, rubbed, and creaked, then made my way, by way of the so-called musical syncopations of Ice Tray, to wakefulness. First order of business, after achieving said blinking consciousness, was a stumble to the john. Not for the first time, staring down into that porcelain mouth, I was puzzled by the fact that this annoying bit of Average Joe biology, of all things, had stayed with me. With a flush, I was also grateful for indoor plumbing. Once you have it, you never, ever want to go back—believe me, especially since back was a very long time ago, when outhouses or just holes in the ground were the order of the day.

Now reasonably aware of my surroundings, I returned to the dimness of my bedroom and started to pick through the pile on the floor, at the foot of my huge bed, hoping for something moderately clean to wear, but willing to settle for "not so smelly as to drop birds from the sky." In the end, I picked out my usual: basic white T, just-right-faded jeans, and a pair of decent running shoes. I might not have a badge, but I had my uniform.

I knew I was in trouble—boy, was I in trouble—but no way in hell was I going to let myself get scared about it, at least not yet. I was cool, I was collected, I was James Dean. If I smoked, I would have lit one up. Instead, I flexed my pecs a bit (not great but definitely not bad, maybe not stone but certainly not flab . . . or much flab), ran a hand through my black curls, and snuggled my ass a bit tighter into my jeans.

Now then, the most important meal of the day. Yum, yum, yum. Bedroom to hall to kitchen. I like my little place. One of the great perks of my internship: a real estate agent who really understood my need as a hip (who I am kidding?), young (as you feel), professional (not quite, but hopefully soon), daylight-challenged hemosapien.

Hardwood floors that only creaked when you walked on them, a kitchen full of the most modern (for 1954) conveniences, plenty of closet space to ignore, wiring that only occasionally smoked and/or sparked, and not a window in the place. One of the best things about it was the piped-in disco, a benefit of being hidden above The Midnight Sun, the Castro's favorite all-night, every night, hot and happening dance spot. Annoying? I'd take rap any time. But it was also kind of comforting to know I was living with something that, just like me, would never, ever die.

But man cannot live by "It's Raining Men" alone. I need more than a good beat you can dance to if *I will survive*. So, breakfast of champions. Into my pale-linoleum and buzzing-fluorescent dining area. I'd say it looked like a morgue but, in this town, that would make my kitchen out to be the Ritz Carlton.

So, door open—fridge light blinking on, twitching and hesitantly waking like I was, its yellowed photons stabbing right into my still-dreamy peepers—I perused for the selection of the day. Luckily I'd been down to the bank the night before and so had a nice little selection of consumables, and to the market the night before that for some stuff to go with it. In the end, just like my jeans and T, I resorted to comfort over spiritually fulfilling or expanding novelty, or the fact that I was obviously, painfully, criminally running late and I was more worried than even I let on and simply couldn't concentrate on originality.

So, a bit of A positive and some Smirnoff. I know what some people say: that for a mixture like this you really have to go for the quality stuff, like some O or B positive, but I and my taste buds just aren't that sophisticated, especially first thing in the morning. Besides, I sure as hell wasn't going to waste the good stuff—what little I had, what little I could afford, on vodka that, with a very little bit of elbow grease, could cut through the most stubborn of crusted-on oven grime.

Finger running around my Fred Flintstone tumbler (broke my Barney years ago), good to the last drop, a remaining smear of red and booze, finger popped into my mouth for a completing suck. Yeah, I was hungry, always that way when I first get up, but even though I was pathologically, totally, completely late it was a final domestic thing before responsibility hauled my taut and shapely cheeks down the stairs, out the door, and off to get that same taut and shapely posterior chewed off. *Sigh,* I say, and did as I put my glass in the sink.

Another benefit of getting access to a realtor who knows where all the city's bodies are buried, and what kind of accommodations they might like to occupy when they get up again, is that they can really put themselves into the shoes (or claws, hooves, suckers, etc.) of their clientele. In my case, after a last-minute trim and fluff in front of the mirror—ah, good as always. Hi there, handsome! Ready to go out and face the night, do your duty and all that shit? Say what you want about the damned but at least we don't have to worry about crow's-feet, wrinkles, pot bellies, receding hairlines, gravity, shrinkage, warping, fading, discoloration, moles, liver spots, arthritis, rampant nose or ear hair (continue with list as it appears between now and coffin time). Oh, sure, there are problems, as well as not really "getting" Geritol, Depends, and AARP commercials, but they all sort of don't matter—at least when you stand in front of the mirror and know that tomorrow, and the day after, and the year after, and the century after, the same grinning moron with the dark curls will be staring back at you.

Mirror? *Mirror?* Ah, yes, I said, you heard, but as my dearly beloved (yes, that's sarcasm) boss would say, or yell, or scream, or bellow, or roar: "WAIT FOR IT, ASSHOLE." Can't spill all my beans right up front, can I? Got to keep some secrets in my pants. Wouldn't do to blow my wad in the first chapter. So I retrieved my jean jacket from the hook by the door and started down the stairs, two at a time as I always do, even though I wasn't at all jazzed about getting where I wanted to go. And then I was at the door.

Steel, thick and solid. Not animal, not vegetable, no doubt mineral. My hand on the handle. Cold metal under my skin. Turn it? Give me a sec.

Sounded like a great idea, a place with no windows, no glass anywhere. Perfect, right? Except that one day I didn't check my clock, assumed (and made an "ass" out of "u" and especially "me"), ran down the stairs as always, put my hand on the knob, turned, opened, and saw the light of a fading day.

No preening after that, no mirror, no "Aren't you a sexy one?" and winking at my reflection. Not for at least a month, thirty or so days of making absolutely sure that there was nothing but cold, dark, glorious night beyond my steel-slab front door.

We heal fast, we damned, but although skin goes smooth from blisters and scars, hair grows back in, and eyes clean from being boiled eggs in cracked sockets, wounds in the brain take a bit longer. That tail end of a bright and sunny day was years ago but still. . . . Hand on knob, chilly alloy sucking at my body heat, I took a slow, steady, and deep breath and opened it slowly, cautiously, stepping behind so if there was an a.m. where I expected p.m. it would show dust motes in the air and a dirty cement landing rather than roasting me like a duck in the window of a Chinese restaurant.

Nothing. No flame of daylight, no warm coals of dusk. I breathed out, weight gone, fear vanishing. Cool air and a few dancing shadows from the normal evening signage of the Castro, plus a few searchlight sweeps from cars gliding down 18th Street.

What a grand Monday night to be . . . well, out and about, at least, if not technically as lusciously warm-blooded as one of the many folks strolling by. Like that one. *Growl.*

And so, turning first to close my secret little door, then back to the dusky loveliness of the ebb and flow of strollers and meanderers of the Castro, I squared my shoulders, put heel to toe, and stepped out toward destiny.

The night was like a wicked magician palming splendor behind a coal-black tuxedo, only revealing color-rich pleasure with a sly gesture of roaming headlights, or with spontaneous bouquets of neon and vibrantly lit plastic enticements.

It was an act I'd seen before, lots of times, but this was the night of the Special Program, a spectacle with nightmares hidden behind the tails of that inky black sleight-of-hand artist, with beasts tucked into his deepest pockets, with things that no one should see, but that I had to, eye to eye—when they had eyes.

The exits were locked for the whole matinee, and that included scratchy newsreel and jerky cartoon short. But I wouldn't have it any other way. Sure, the newsreel would chew you up and stick you under a seat. Yeah, the headliner would suck you dry as British wit then ever so politely ask for a breath mint, and even the cartoon short would drive a stake in your heart, but I was right there, front row, center.

I was more than ready. I was absolutely willing, I was able and then some, and I had my popcorn: Time to get this show on the road.

Who am I kidding? I tripped on a crack in the sidewalk and fell flat on my face.

Getting up, dusting off, I headed out: late for work. Very late for work.

II

Ah, insane Frisco, Baghdad by the bay, where the men are separated from the boys . . . with a crowbar or, my favorite—and I can bet you know why—sanguine by the sea. Been a lot of places during my crimson-prolonged existence on this spinning ball of mud and rock and I can tell you up-front and honest, scout's honor, that there's no better place to be, whether you're a special brand of sucker (like me) or just your run-of-the-mill, garden-variety froot loop (a registered trademark of whatever corporation owns Froot Loops).

Down Castro Street, nods to the hustle, smiles to the bustle (especially his). A lovely fall night, atmosphere charged with possibility, air fragrant with potential—a night for sweet drinks, a waltzing flirtation, a two-step with the eyes, and then . . . well, use your imagination.

I certainly did. Of course, that's because that's all I was using, the best of my bod being sorely neglected in the flirtation, two-stepping, and wherever it could lead.

Sure, I'm not exactly Abercrombie catalog material but I'm not *that* hard to look at. At least my primping mirror hasn't cracked—yet. Let's just say that my problem with meeting and having a successful relationship with the same sex has less to do with my visage and more to do with the inherent age difference between me and my intendeds, dietary needs and social circles notwithstanding.

That doesn't mean I don't put myself out there into the black lagoon of poppers, pills, pot, and . . . some kind of booze that starts with "p," rather than ending with it. Yes, you may laugh; that was a good one. But you know what it was like before you came out (that is, if you've come out). "I'm the only one" (sob), "No one will understand" (whimper), "I'm weird" (sniffle), "I'm a freak" (boo-hoo). Well, I could be in a testosterone-fogged club, nothing but chiseled chests, leering dental work, hoses unreeling everywhere, and I'd still feel that way,

The Very Bloody Marys

doi:10.1300/5329_02

because there's no two ways about it—I'm all that and a helluva lot more. Except for human, that is. Haven't been that for a loooong time.

Oh, sure, there was always the possibility of the horizontal bump, or even the vertical hustle, or the sideways froug, with a fellow sucker or other differently abled, sunlight-challenged individual, but, well, have you seen some of them? Of course you haven't, and for a damned good reason. Not that all of them are the stuff of public works legend or cemetery tall tale, but let's just say that even in that arena my batting average is not going to get me into the majors, or even the minors. Okay, let's be honest: I've struck out there as well.

So, down Castro to Market, waiting for the Black Mariah, scanning for the cab as well as a friendly smile, everyone holding hands or kissing right out there in public. Notice how you hate public displays when you have no one to publicly display with? A night of potential and possibility, passing me by—one more time.

Okay, enough of that shit. I had a job to do—or a job I was really late for. That made the evening even more complete: not only strolling through pairs and pairs and quads and quads and group gropes of happy guys (and a few scattered gals and straight combos) but I was late, really late, damned late, incredibly late.

Pogue was gonna be pissed.

Market Street, the glowing consumerism of Crate and Barrel making me smile. I still remember the fuss and bother when it was put in, no one but me and a few select other folks remembering that other fuss, those other bothers when Walgreens, BofA, Starbucks, the gas station, the theater, the streetcar, the underground went in. Sometimes I can still see all that, blinking time lapse walking around the city. One eyelid down and the cars are all fat and chrome, the ladies in skirts; with the other closed, it's cobblestones and horseshit. Nostalgic but, believe me, you don't want to live in the past after you've had indoor plumbing or stepped into one of Flicka's steamers.

Finally, there he was: another perk of my hard (hardly) working (as little as possible) life. A less-than-hansom cab, yellow as pissholes in a snowbank. Tell you, no matter how many rides I'd taken with him, I still shuddered when he drove up. A gift from an ancient, and I hope very dead practitioner of Italian voodoo, the Mariah was our official/

unofficial way of getting from here to there in the city. "Here" being where I was, "there" being my boss's place.

Sliding into the back, I gave him a destination in what I hoped was clear, concise English ("Take me to Pogue's") and tried to settle in for the ride. The machine was ancient and battered, the springs as dead and no doubt mushy as the driver. As usual, I tried to keep my eyes off the back of his glossy black head, especially the Braille of zits sprayed over the rolls of sagging head fat, and especially away from the rear-view window. One time—big shudder here—I had caught a look at his eyes, two puss-filled boiled-egg eyes staring, unblinking, straight ahead, and didn't sleep well for a week. Momma Mia sure could make them, rest her heretical soul. When they died they stayed dead—and on the job.

Pogue was *really* going to be pissed.

I also almost told my lively (hardly) cabby to pull over, let me out. I'd take a walk, that's what I do, something I hadn't done for a long time. And when I say a long time you know I mean a long, long, long time. Take a stroll, that's what I'd do. Just step out of the car and see what this lovely night had to offer. A club, perhaps? A great meal, maybe? When's the last time I had good pasta? How about a bar full of pounding bass and swinging hips? A pair of lovely eyes—finally—to stare into? Lay out on the grass in some park and watch the stars roll and wheel overhead? A kiss—a great and true and honest and hot kiss?

But I didn't. You'd think after all this time I'd be braver, be able to look that buzz-cutted bastard right in the eye and tell him to perform some anatomically impossible act of self-penetration. But I couldn't. It wasn't for lack of wanting to, you understand. Pogue was a bastard, pure and simple, without question, but I was stuck with him—until he was done with me, and so far, at this rate, that wasn't going to be for a very, very, very long time.

And, again, you know that means a very, very, very . . . and hating every goddamned second of it.

A stoplight. I looked up, trying to figure out where I was and how much time before we got to North Beach. A donut place on the corner, home to the losers of the economic wars, victims of needles and bottles. Ah, the heart of the city, a few blocks from city hall. Van Ness. A few minutes before I would be there. Time to put together an excuse.

"Goddamn it, you pantywaist fuckwad! Are you too fucking stupid you can't tell the fucking time!"

Well, sir, Pogue, sir, it was like this: I was back in my authorized residence, domicile if you will, putting a crease you could cut yourself with on my dress pants when all of a sudden—and I do mean all of a sudden, sir—I was attacked by the Sudanese Demon of Salt and Tears, and I should not have to tell you, sir, how vicious one of those SOBs can be, especially in the early evening when most people aren't crying their eyes out or taking lots of salt with their meals. Luckily, or should I say because of my superior training at your capable hands, sir, I was able to defeat this particular manifestation of transdimensional supreme evil through the correct and expert application of a sugar substitute (the blue stuff, of course, not the pink) and some non-dairy creamer (the nonfat kind, naturally). And may I say, sir, that the battle was a great one but obviously, as I am here, albeit a little late, that I prevailed against this ferocious creature from the Beyond. Evidence, sir? Well, um, er, ah, you know how awfully . . . um, aromatic a dead Sudanese Demon of Salt and Tears can be, especially after being professionally and thoroughly dispatched by your own proscribed methodology, and rather than bring such a foul carcass into your quarters, I instead . . . um, flushed it down the toilet . . . after cutting it up into pieces . . . with a chainsaw that I just happened to have laying around . . . my apartment.

"You fucking piece of useless goddamn undead garbage. Can't you even tell what fucking time it is?"

There I was putting my shoes on when I suddenly realized—shock, amazement, dismay—that my left was where my right should be. "Ah," I thought to myself, "this reminds me of something that the Great and Powerful Pogue was telling me just the other day, about how the wee folk haven't made an appearance in our little berg by the bay for well over a century and how this kind of thing—left foot for right foot—was just the kind of thing those diminutive beer-and-potatoes mischief makers would do." Immediately recognizing this threat from the other side of the pond, I desperately tried to recall your instructions about how to dismiss such a threat. Unfortunately, I was plum out of Lucky Charms and my Riverdance tape was stuck in the VCR, so I had to re-

sort to a can of Boston baked beans, which I used to repeatedly and rather forcefully bludgeon the wee creature into a barely recognizable mass of twitching mythology, which I then neatly bagged and dropped in the nearest "specialized" dumpster for "authorized" sanitation. That's why I'm late, sir: I had to run down to Walgreens to pick up some of those extra sturdy lawn and leaf bags. Didn't want him, or should I say the body . . . leaking, you know . . . all over the carpet.

"You're fucking scum! Goddamn fucking scum! How fucking dare you show up two fucking hours late!"

I tell ya, sir, it came out of nowhere. A roaring beast it was, all tooth and fang and claw and mean as the meanest sin there ever was—and you know how mean that can be. I used every trick you taught me but it kept coming. It bit me, it chewed on me, it tore at me, but it just wasn't enough. As I felt those teeth bite, those fangs chew, those claws tear, I knew that this was it, the end, game over, il finito—but then the weirdest thing happened: Just as it was going to pull me apart and swallow me down its fuming and steamy gullet, I heard this voice in my head, louder, bellowing with an even greater rage: "Get up, you goddamned undead faggot!" And that's what I did, sir, that's just what I did. I got up off my damn belly and faced the thing, stared it right in its glistening eyes and damn but I didn't scream right into its gleaming, squirming what-passed-for-a-face: "Fuck you! FUCK YOU! I'm not scared of you, 'cause I've been kicked in the ass by the devil himself: Pogue!" I don't know if it was my yelling, or your name, sir, but that creature didn't stick around. It turned right around and ran off with its tail between its legs. God's truth, that's why I'm late.

Then I was there, or should I say that's when I realized Mariah had pulled over. Shaking my head, I looked out the cab window at the pale brick ghosts standing at parade rest up and down the narrow street, the dark lines of their fire escapes hanging on their fronts like medals for architectural boredom. Welcome to North Beach.

Mariah drove off, leaving me standing in front of beveled glass doors, under an awning of filigreed iron. I was late. I was very late, but I didn't go in—at least not yet. Instead, I just stood there, staring miserably at the brass and plastic call box, at the one button marked with a tiny slip of yellowed and stained paper in particular: POGUE.

My boss. His voice rang in my ears as my finger hovered over the button:

"You miserable fucking excuse for a goddamn vampire. Two hundred fucking years on this fucking planet and you still can't show up on fucking time!"

Well, funny you should mention that, SIR, but I was just thinking about the very same thing this evening as I was getting all primed and proper in preparation to run down here just so I could spend another night in your oh-so-pleasant company. See, it's like this, SIR: I am a fucking idiot, as you so eloquently and repeatedly put it. A waste of time, vampiric trash, undead crap, supernatural-shit-that-walks. That's me. Yup, that's me.

I didn't want to push that button. I really didn't want to push that button. But you know what? I did. One flex of a tiny muscle, one tug of a tendon and my fingerprint was on a rectangle of plastic next to POGUE. The purr of a dialing phone scratched out of a speaker somewhere.

I didn't have a choice. No heroics, no strength of character—just no other option. Sure, I could stretch out on the tickling chill of a city park at midnight, watch the stars move across the deep, dark sky. Take in a show. Feast on something exotic and expensive. Stare longingly into a pair of eyes. Hold someone's hand. A kiss, mixing heats outside a rocking nightclub. I could do all that: hand in my resignation, walk away from Pogue, tell the boss to *fuck off*.

The phone wasn't ringing anymore. Just a dial tone. I punched Pogue again, heard the connection. The phone rang once again.

No boss, no job, no money. No money, no blood—and those days of nibbles on throats, fresh and hot and salty straight from the neck, were long gone, for me and for every other sucker in the city or the whole damned world.

So, there I was, two hours late, putting my head in the crocodile's mouth, waiting for it to be bitten off.

But . . . ring, ring, ring, and then another dial tone.

Where was he?

III

Ring, ring, ring—dial tone. Ring, ring, ring—dial tone. Ring, ring, ring—dial tone. Ring, ring, ring—dial tone. Ring, ring, ring—dial tone.

I checked my nails, found them clean enough, but just to be on the safe side, slid thumb one under index two to work loose a sliver of dark something-or-other.

Ring, ring, ring—dial tone. Ring, ring, ring—dial tone. Ring, ring, ring—dial tone. Ring, ring, ring—dial tone. Ring, ring, ring—dial tone.

I looked up the street: hesitant islands of light from feeble streetlamps, bright bursts of headlights as cars rolled up the hill, red astrophenomena from brakes as others headed down. Brighter pools from lobbies like mine (temporary occupation) or Pogue's (permanent occupation). The sky was full of rectangular stars; constellations not of bulls, bears, rams, or girls with bow-and-arrow fetishes but instead of who was home and who wasn't, who had lives and who was hiding from them. Some, I noticed in my dull concentration, were flickering from TV radiation, and I realized I had no idea what was on right now.

Ring, ring, ring—dial tone. Ring, ring, ring—dial tone. Ring, ring, ring—dial tone. Ring, ring, ring—dial tone. Ring, ring, ring—dial tone.

Bored. Time to go through my wallet: Two twenties, one five, and seven ones. Of those, one twenty, not the five, and only three of the ones had that subtle aroma of Blood Money (hot pennies and pretzels, I always thought whenever I sniffed Abe, Jackson, or Washington). In American currency, I was almost broke; in that other form of exchange I was most definitely bankrupt. Crap. Looked like I'd be sipping the cheap red rather than any finer vintages. At least I had a job. At least I *hoped* I had a job. Was this that buzz-cut, blood-sucking asshole's way of pink-slipping me?

Ring, ring, ring—dial tone. Ring, ring, ring—dial tone. Ring, ring, ring—dial tone. Ring, ring, ring—dial tone. Ring, ring, ring—dial tone.

The Very Bloody Marys

doi:10.1300/5329_03

Nah. Say what you wanted about the U.S. Army's finest undead, but this just wasn't Pogue's style. He'd roar, scream, bellow, rage, and slam his fist into my oh-so-tender stomach; but just not answer the door? No sense. No dollars, either. Man, I hated the cheap stuff.

Where the hell was he? Pogue had less of a social life than I did. Two years of "Sir, yes, sir," "Sir, no, sir," and a bunch of other sentences all starting with sir and ending with sir, and I knew two things about Pogue: jack and shit. Well, that's not completely true . . . sir! I know you have no life, sir! I know you were always here, sir! Even if I was late, sir! No sick days, sir! Because we never get sick, sir!

Ring, ring, ring—dial tone. Ring, ring, ring—dial tone. Ring, ring, ring—dial tone. Ring, ring, ring—dial tone. Ring, ring, ring—dial tone.

So where the hell are you—sir?

Doubt, worry, anger, even a bit of joy (a night off!) followed by bargaining: Okay, gonna give the asshole twenty more minutes before walking away. Twenty minutes before the employee, trainee, student, intern, apprentice, me, Valentino, takes a few well-chosen strides down the street.

Then a darker shade of shadow, a velvet swatch of night, a darker bit of darkness, a bit of charcoal painted on soot peeled away from the recesses of a service doorway. Inside the raven wing, the opaque, a face, and, on that face, a sly smile. Out of the sly smile, a scintillating voice, a melodic sing-song in a whispering contralto: "*Bonjour,* Monsieur Valentino. *C'est un plaisir* to see you!"

Central Casting, send up Maurice Chevalier, Louis Jordan, Claude Rains, or—if you're into rough trade—Jean Reno. Stick them in an ebony suit sewn up with ink, stick a wide-brimmed fedora dark as 2:00 a.m. (which it wasn't yet) on his head and tilt it just so: a last-minute touch of the stylish, the roguish, a pinch of menace, a dash of slick cool.

To which I said, "H-hello." Not to the hat—to the guy. To which I thought, also not to the hat: *Oh, crap*. "N-nice to meet you." *Just what I need.*

"*Oui, enchante,* sir. *Sacre bleu,* my manners. Forgive me, I am. . . . Well, why do you not simply address me as Monsieur Ombre?"

"Hombre?"

"Ah, you make a small joke!" Laughing but not really laughing. "No, it is said 'Ombre.'"

"Ombree?"

"No, no. *Ombre*. Be aware of the mouth: *Oooo*m-bray. You should roll the letters. *Oooo*m-bray."

"Omber?"

"Merde," he said, head back, eyes to the stars, a plea of patience to a distant silver-dollar moon. Gleaming eyes back toward me: "Two hundred years and you still cannot *parlez vous le Francais*?"

"Well, yeah, but you still have that accent—however old you are?" I said, trying to play a cool hand but knowing my fingers were quivering more than a little.

I hoped I didn't flinch or step back when his brows tilted together and his face crawled into a stern frown. I hoped my wallet would suddenly be bulging with crisp, high-denomination bills. I hoped Pogue would appear, stepping out of his lobby, strolling down the street, with a smile (imagine it! a smile!), a slap on my back, and a hearty chortle (imagine it! a chortle!) at seeing me there. I hoped this damned color-challenged French individual would fade back into the shadows and leave me the hell alone.

But, honestly, my wallet was still just two twenties, one five, and seven ones (U.S.) with just one twenty and three ones that reminded me of hot New York nights and wonderful yellow mustard. Pogue was still AWOL, and Monsieur Ombre (I can spell it even if I can't pronounce it) was still glaring at me.

But then he laughed. Okay, it wasn't a from-the-gut chortle or even a sneeze of amusement but, hell, at that point I'd take what I could get.

"Okay, you got me there," he said. *Gladys, get on the horn to Central and have them send up Eastwood, Wayne, Cooper, or Rogers, but not if he wants to bring that damned horse.* The kind of guy, in other words, who would say Hombre and not *Ombre*. The frown turned upside down and a hand extended from the deep, dark depths of his ink and shade and shadow cloak.

I shook it, trying to return the smile as best I could. I liked the change in his tone—and accent—but I didn't like what was going on.

Where the hell was Pogue? I shouldn't be dealing with this guy. Pogue was the boss; he should be the one chatting with a rep from the home office.

"So . . ." this hombre said, "have you seen Pogue lately?"

"Last I saw of him was Friday. Business as usual. Nothing since then, I'm afraid. Nothing suspicious. Nothing out of the ordinary. Just Pogue and I—and you know Pogue, regular as clockwork. But then you might not know Pogue. But, believe me, he is as regular as . . . clockwork. Maybe I should stop talking now."

"Well . . . yes, he's kind of legendary in the punctuality department, which is why it's so odd that no one has seen him since you did, last Friday."

"He seemed fine, you know? Very Pogueish in that Pogueish kind of way he does so well. Nobody can do Pogue like he can. Kind of an expert, you could say, in Pogueism."

"Um, yes. You see, it's very important that I locate him. We'd asked him to look into possible illegal activity." A beat, waiting for the suspense to build. "A transformation."

Shit, I thought. "Shit," I said. I may not have my badge yet (so what if night cops didn't get badges?) but I knew his news was bad, very bad. "That's bad," I said, demonstrating my brains and ability once again.

"It is. Very bad. We believe the initiator was an Australian named DeAngeles, himself an illegal, as a result of a sloppy feed in Melbourne. He'd stowed away in a container ship."

What a trip. Just the thought of it gave me goose bumps: weeks in a dark, stinking hold, munching on rats and maybe, if he was careful or desperate enough, one of the crew. A newbie as well, not knowing what was going on, trying to remember every damned book, movie, or TV show, trying to understand the rules. That first blister, or burn from daylight. The first cross and not feeling a thing. The first *hello* to his own face in a mirror or maybe just a bit of polished bulkhead. Managing—barely—to make it all the way to the city, trying to deal with what had happened, what he had become. *Christ.*

"Pogue managed to 'remove' him several weeks ago but there is suspicion on his and the *Conseil*'s part that DeAngeles had transformed others."

"Christ" was right. Yeah, weeks of sucking rats, discovering that sunlight is bad, that blood is good, that crosses mean shit, that stakes are for eating. Then off that boat from Australia. A whole city of people to see, people to drink.

Then a day, maybe even just a few hours later, a guy with short-shorn hair, gun-barrel-tight eyes, firm jaw set and rock hard, spine straighter than a Baptist preacher's, a steel-strong hand out in greeting: "Welcome to San Francisco, son. Sorry your visit is gonna be a short one."

Accidental vampire, meet Pogue, the last face you're ever going to see.

I shook my head to get the image out, tried to focus on what Mr. Ombre was saying. "Oh, shit. Oh, crap. Oh, fuck. How many?"

He shook his head, inky hat swinging back and forth. "No idea. Pogue was handling the investigation. I'm only in town as a *Conseil* liaison. He didn't tell you anything of this?"

Well, Monsieur Ombre, let me impart unto you what I've learned from my employer and mentor of these many years. Let me speak to you of the knowledge brought down from the highest mountain peaks of wisdom by the U.S. Army's very best vampiric drill sergeant. I shall regale you with data and information, techniques and methodologies, legend and myth, particulars and facts of the Between Places, the Sideways Lands, the Other Worlds, the Shady Kingdoms, the Flipsides, the Alternations.

Sit down, for this may take a while.

Okay, Pogue really did cram as much as possible into my tiny little brain. Sometimes I swear I lay awake at day. . . . Weird, isn't it, how some things just don't translate? Anyway, I'd lie awake and try to keep what he'd told me from leaking out onto my pillow. Sure, I'd stare off into space on occasion, desperately attempting to remember whether this beastie, creature, thing, demon, god, monster, or a mixture of any of the above had to be dealt with in this or that fashion—or just left the hell alone. Absolutely, I've picked up a trick or two over the long, long, long years as Pogue's assistant, disciple, trainee, or just "fucking loser asshole, no-good, fucking waste of fucking undead life!"

But if there is one thing I know for sure, that I am absolutely sure of, it's that Pogue would never, ever tell me everything. On my good nights (another weird phrase there), I'd tell myself that we still had plenty of time for this lesson or that bit of information to be imparted, that there were many lessons still to be taught, lots of procedures and strategies remaining to be passed on from boss to employee. *After all,* I'd say to myself when I had a swagger in my step and I was holding my head up high, *what's a few years compared to a few hundred?* He'd get around to it . . . eventually.

But when my chin was on my chest, when I tripped and fell flat on my face right out of the door, when I overslept, was broke, or late, I knew that the real reason Pogue simply kept things from me was because . . . well, would you gift a fucked-up creature like myself with the whole picture? Of course you wouldn't.

Fucked up or not, creature or not, I sure as hell wasn't going to let Monsieur Ombre from the *Conseil* know that. *Fucking loser asshole, no-good, fucking waste of fucking undead life* is one thing; *really stupid* is another.

"Oh, yes—I think I recall this situation now. The Austrian, DeAngelo, the 'removal' of him. It's all coming back to me now. You know what a wild and crazy place San Francisco can be. Just slipped my mind is all."

"Australian."

"Excuse me?"

"The initiator of the transformation. He was Australian, not Austrian, and his name was DeAngeles, not DeAngelo."

"Whatever," I said with a wave of my hand. "I'm sure Pogue is working on the situation right now. More than likely he thought it was just too, well, minor for him to involve me in the actual pursuit."

"Did Pogue mention the Very Bloody Marys?"

"Why should he?"

"Merde," he said, soft and light. "The body of a young man was found in an alley near Polk Street. Initial reports indicate he'd been fed on, after Pogue had eliminated DeAngeles."

"Ah, yes. It's coming back to me: blond, about twenty-five . . ."

"Dark haired, about eighteen."

"Close to Clay—"

"Near Geary—"

"His last words were 'Bloody Marys'—"

"Painted on the wall of the alley, in the victim's blood."

"I'm screwed, aren't I?" I said, looking down at the sidewalk, my cheap tennis shoes. One, I noticed to my further embarrassment, was untied. No wonder I'd fallen flat on my face.

The hat dipped down as well and I wondered for a moment if he, too, was noticing my lace flapping in the breeze. *Here it comes,* I thought: the whish of the axe, the pink of the slip. Goodbye, idea of fine hemoglobin, and hello, trying to get out of town before the *Conseil* snaps its fingers and sends out another Ombre, this one with the gun-barrel eyes, coiled-spring muscles, and the granite bones of Pogue. One hand out, the other behind his back, hiding something heavy and sharp.

Two hundred years. It'd been a good run. Lots of . . . well, there'd been blood, of course. Moons. Stars. Rain. Fog. Hiding, too: all-night movie theaters, bars, discos, stables, warehouses, churches, a few synagogues (even a mosque or two), schools (during the summer), my own fair share of ships and their holds—places dark and secret and, I'd hoped at the time, safe.

Lots of . . . I was going to say friends but, to be honest, the nightlife might be advantageous to boogying but it doesn't make for long-term relationships. Some back-alley assignations, sticky stuff in my mouth or on my shirt or pants; not blood, or at least not up until a few years ago.

Two hundred sure sounds like a lot, but . . . the time just seemed to have hopped, skipped, and jumped by. Never skied, never sailed, never surfed, never had two guys at once, never fished, never painted a picture, never wrote a poem, never flew a kite, never been to a picnic, never wore a tux, never went to a flower show, never—well, it's a long list.

What surprised me the most, though, was that I wanted more: orchids, bow ties, potato salad, string, oil or watercolor, hooks and line, two of everything, boards, anchors, poles, and all the rest. Never knew what you really might be missing until you were close to losing it, I guess.

I was set to bolt, to turn tail and run (stopping abruptly to tie my shoelace) and make for the border (what border, I had no idea; the *Conseil* was everywhere there was blood and those who drink it), when Monsieur Ombre's black hat eclipse retreated as he lifted his head, showing an unreadable expression on his cast-of-thousands face.

"Monsieur Valentino," he said, French without the accent, accidental or intentional slip back into official pretension, I couldn't tell. "It's essential that this situation be investigated. If there has been another unauthorized transformation then it must be dealt with. I'm the *Conseil* on this matter, and we say that if Pogue is working on this situation then he must be located immediately."

"Hey, I can do that. No problem!" I said, the axe lifting off the back of my shapely neck.

"But if something has happened to prevent Pogue from fulfilling his responsibilities, then it is your duty to take on the investigation—unless you feel that you are unable to do this?"

"Oh, no—I mean, yes. I mean, sure, I can do that. You can count on me."

"Good. I will contact you again soon."

Ombre means, basically, to be obscured by darkness, and that's just what he did, fading back, melting into the soft velvet of the night. There one moment, gone the next. There were two of us, and then it was me. Just me.

I knew I didn't know much. Yes, you read that right. Sure, there were gaps in my education, things that Pogue had neglected to tell me, was waiting for just the right moment to teach me, was never ever going to pass along, but I did know some simple, direct, and obvious things. Things like my next sunrise would be my last, that I love A positive with Smirnoff, that twenty percent is a standard tip, that

Barbra can turn every note on the scale to pure magic, that I don't look good in drag (don't ask), and one all-important, essential fact pertaining to that moment in my life: I was really, profoundly, totally, and absolutely screwed.

IV

Shit. Or should I say *merde*? No, shit it was, and in it I was, up to my pearly whites, my two pointed teeth. Thing about *merde,* you see, was it is a bit too close for comfort. French comfort. Shit, though, that was pure English, all American.

Small victories: Take that, *Le Conseil Carmin*.

So, standing on a cold street, the starlight of windows all the way to the rooftops, with real starlight even higher. Distant suns, just dancing pinpoints in deep velvet. All the daylight I'd ever see.

Where the fuck was Pogue?

Without really thinking about it, I knew that Mariah would be cruising up in a moment or three, dead eyes sunk into shoe-polished leather skin, unblinking and unspeaking. Like I said, perks of the job: affordable nourishment, disco-thumping accommodations, an abusive and now AWOL superior, and a ride to wherever you needed to go.

So where did I need to go?

Thinking of Mariah brought up the job, the job brought up French, French brought up *Le Conseil Carmin,* the *Conseil* brought up blood, and blood always brought up history. Doesn't it always?

Okay, kids: Have a seat. Here comes a bit of exposition: History was never my best subject, even though I've lived through a helluva lot of it, but this I knew very well. They made sure of that.

But a long time ago, even before my time, and that's a whole lot of years, there wasn't a "they" at all. Just a bunch of snots and snobs with nothing to do but lay around all night and sip fine vintages, nibble on delicacies, trade witticisms—chuckling at the better jokes, smacking at the better tidbits, and making sophisticated yummy noises over the better bottles. Oh, sure, we all know they had poor roots, these nouveau nosferatu, those bucktoothed, backwoods, bat-winged *things* that had drifted down from their usual Transylvanian hunting grounds

The Very Bloody Marys

doi:10.1300/5329_04

when the goats got a bit too . . . well, "goaty" for their tastes. But that was ages ago, and they'd moved up in the world, or at least into a better address.

It was all warm, salty vintages; supple necks of the choicest of morsels for a long time. "I say, Marcel, what's better than being a vampire?" "I don't know, Louie, what is better than being a vampire?" "Why nothing, you silly." Guffaw, guffaw, guffaw, chortle, snort.

But take one snotty bore and multiply, multiply, multiply, multiply, multiply, multiply (bunnies have nothing on reckless bloodsuckers) and you can see the problem. One Marcel is bad enough, but a whole Paris of them is a colossal pain in the neck. So to speak.

Flip a couple of pages in certain books and it was just a peasant uprising—chop, chop, chop of Madame Guillotine. That old broad knitting one, pearling two, as the noggins go rolling into wicker baskets. But that was in daylight. When the sun had gone down, it was a smarter bunch of vamps who'd seen the problem as more than just a city overpopulated with Marcels and Louies. These vamps were a bit more forward-thinking than that. A city of chortling and snorting bloodsuckers was bad enough, but what happens when those fine vintages, all those lovely necks, are all gone, when those tidbits have all been bitten?

Flip a couple of pages in certain other musty tomes and it was anything *but* a peasant uprising. Oh, sure, a lot of blue bloods had theirs spilled on dirty Parisian cobblestones, but a lot of more literally societal parasites had lost theirs at daylight, adding much desiccated powder to those winding streets. They and their lives of *hoi* and *polloi* went up in puffs of smoke.

Citizens ran things after that: butlers and gardeners, nannies and nurses, schoolteachers and sweepers, clearing the slate of anything noble, or at least titled. Lots of bare-breasted solitary symbols waving flags. In the day, at least. When the sun set on the new Republic, it was time for the twilight revolutionaries to get to work. Out with the bad blood, in with the new.

Le Conseil Carmin: Call it what you will, but never in English. They're still touchy about that, even two hundred years after staking out their new regime.

But their purging didn't stop with the romantic snail shell we (and they) call *Parie*. Oh, no. I said they had vision, right? Well, their eyes saw all over the globe and, with the help of early nasties like my Monsieur Ombre, they went from Pole to Pole and even to Poland, bringing their rivals and other wild vamps to light. Poof!

Me? I was lucky. More on that later.

So, in power and really damned pleased with themselves, they set up their little empire. Letting the other little human revolutionaries get on with their Terror, picking up the pieces after. Hey, blood is blood, and it was a good way to get some nice meals and also to make sure that when it was all over they were not only on top of their vampire world but also with those other poor saps . . . homo saps, if you know what I mean.

I told you these folks were forward-thinking. Let the vamps feed and feed and feed and you have nothing but starving vamps and no humans to feed on; hence their population-control program. And what do Mr. And Mrs. Average Joe Human get out of it?

Look in the shadows and what do you see? Shade, right? Anything but light. Soft dark, deep-black velvet. Look through it though, right in that shifting haze where one becomes the other, bright to dusk, dawn to night, and you might see something staring back at you, running greasy tongue over needle-sharp teeth. Hungry, those things are. Nasty, those things are. You think Count this or that, Marcel and Louie, or even shaggy little me with my incisors and ability to burn rather than tan is scary? You think big, mean, loud, Pogue is scary? You think the lifeless stare of Mariah is scary?

Look in the shadows, buddy. They're there. Believe me. I've seen them. Well, Pogue told me about them, and when he did, when that stiff-straight, bayonet ramrod, full-metal-jacket bastard did, I saw in his gleaming gunmetal eyes just a quaver, maybe a touch, could have even been a good solid hint of . . . okay, maybe not fear, per se, but for him it had been close enough.

Yes, you may shudder. I sure as hell did.

So, in the city of lights, after dark, a bunch of smart-ass vamps sit and proclaim, rule and dictate, pushing castles and knights across a board, planning it all. And because they can't be anywhere, they have their own little cadre of Monsieur Ombres to do the dirty work. Or, when the work isn't all that messy, or is just plain dull, there are legions of vamps like my Pogue, *Le Corps Policier Contre*.

This is where I come in. When it's even duller than dull, taking no talent or skill, you pass it off to the trainee. "Hi. My name is Valentino and I'm going to be your vampire tonight. Do you want fries with that?"

Fries. Food. This is where my belly comes in: Job means Blood Money, the smelly (to us vamps) currency we use to buy what we need, a vintage O positive or a pull-tab A, to keep me and the rest of us vamps happy, healthy, and undead. That's the way of the world, folks: *Le Conseil Carmin* keeps the biggest, baddest, nastiest of the biggest, baddest, nastiest critters, demons, daemons, monsters, devils, gnomes, banshees, jinn, Sheols, beasts, shades, specters, howlers, eaters, screamers, and schemers content. And, sure, you can thank us for this diligence and fighting the good fight against these really mean and really nasty "things in the shadows," but you already have.

Ever given blood? Thanks for the finely flavored O positive and the trailer-park A, folks. Means a lot to me, or my belly (and those of the rest of the diligent vamps). Got to watch out for our food supply, right? So you bleed and we keep an eye on the dark corners. Works for us, and—believe me—a pint here or there is a lot better than dealing with some of those tooth-and-claw things Pogue told me about between bouts of abuse and comments about my worth to the organization, the world as a whole, or even my value as fertilizer for petunia bulbs (which is not a great deal, according to him).

So, you bleed, we eat. We protect and you . . . well, you bleed, and we eat, and the world turns round and round. It may not be perfect, but you're around, we're around, and if things work out well and I don't screw up too much, I like it. Better than turning into the end of a well-smoked filter tip with the first rays of morning.

Now, now, I know what you're thinking. Oh, that's what it's like, to be a member of the undead, the vamp folk, the suckers and their friends—and you'd be almost right. But did you catch that? "Almost." When I got changed, turned, made, killed, and brought back, we didn't have torrid paperbacks or Saturday morning matinees with

Bella rising from his pine box and asking for a drink, anything but wine. Nah, when I got bit, we were lucky to have a fire, let alone Bella and his creatures of the night. More later on me and how I got from Point A (there) to Point B (here), but let me say that when I first made it into one of those late, late, late shows with Bella up on the big silver screen, or got my hands on my first book with a chap with a toothy smile and a cape on the cover, I was more than a bit surprised by how much they got wrong.

Garlic, for instance. Okay, the appetite for anything but real fine, "right from the neck" brews might be a bit on the faded side, but for a long time there was nothing better on my plate than perfectly cooked pasta (al dente, if you have to ask) some olive oil, and a few choice slivers of that wonderful bulb.

Silver's another: gaudy, to be sure, but as far as "GACK! GASP! NO! ANYTHING BUT THAT!" it's about as scary as over-boiling your pasta.

Sleeping in coffins? How creepy is that? Give me a nice big bed—feathers or springs—any time. Silk sheets, if I could afford them (and I couldn't). No wonder some of the ones on the screen and in those paperbacks were always in a nasty temper. Give them a nice room and a comfy mattress and I'll bet they wouldn't go biting anyone's head off (unless they were hungry, of course—goes without saying).

Crosses? Holy water? Crucifixes? Hosts? Yawn and yawn again. Unless, of course, we're talking a real bit of whim-wham, a serious item of hocus-pocus, an honest device of legerdemain, then I'd be making an ash out of myself (nyuck, nyuck). Luckily, the folks with these kinds of hobbies are usually on our side, as the things that really go bump in the after hours don't like any kind of edge on them floating around in anyone else's hands, hooves, claws, and tentacles. Not to say that mystical run-ins aren't part of the job, but stumbling over an occasional Christ on his cross, bit of mumbled-over tap water, Star of David, or crescent moon and star isn't going to do anything nasty to yours truly.

Changing into bats, wolves, wolverines, hedgehogs, gerbils, hamsters, pigeons, ferrets, puppies, kitties, dolphins, gorillas, goldfish, crabs, eagles, snakes, lizards, fleas, spiders, raccoons, gazelles, lions, tigers, bears, baboons, lemurs, walking sticks, jellyfish, whales, tuna, cod, mackerel, flounder, cows, pigs, chickens? Nope. I'm just me. Though Pogue did know one trick: Piss him off in just the right, or wrong, way, and he'd turn into a real asshole.

Stakes? Well, I'm not going to go out and try that any time soon, but according to that soft-spoken, nurturing, supportive, kind, and contentious font of wisdom that is Pogue, a hammer and a bit of wood would, in his soft-spoken, nurturing, supportive, kind, and contentious words "hurt like a fucking motherfucker, asshole!" As far as he said and I knew, it would do the job. But then, other things would as well.

I tell ya, Buffy (and the other hot, hot, hot boy Scoobies) didn't really need to haul out the heavy medieval machinery to take out night people such as myself. Sure, we might be able to take a lot more hits and cuts and stabs and burns than folks who can work on their tans, but chop off my head (OUCH!), punch a mean old wooden spike into my romantic beater (OUCH!), set me on fire (OUCH!), drop me from the top of a tall pit of architecture (OUCH!), hit me with a big enough truck (OUCH!) and that, my boss the philosopher would say, would be "the end of your miserable fucking life, turdball."

Sunlight? Ah, there we go. Poof, poof, poof. Haven't seen the sun for two hundred years and hope not to see it again. Miss it? Well, I used to be a tan young lad, but now I'm just a tad on the side of pasty. Not a great life, maybe, but it sure beats dying. So, as a handy reference:

Garlic: Tasty
Running water: Have a nice swim
Sleeping in coffins: Uncomfortable
Crosses: Yawn
Transformation: Nope
Stakes: Ouch!
Sunlight: Poof!

Got that? There'll be a quiz tomorrow. Ten points each on the fill-in, fifteen on the oral (ha ha ha), essay question ("What it means to be a vampire") is twenty, multiple choice is twenty-five, and the math portion is . . . whatever percentage points are left over because I haven't the faintest idea. I might drink blood but I can't count to twenty with my shoes on.

So there we are, and there I was, standing outside Pogue's little apartment, no sign of my boss. My job to find him, and stop the Very Bloody Marys. Great, just great. Breathe in, breathe out. "You can do this, you can do this, you can do this, you can do this, you can do this, you can do this": the mantra of the insecure and desperate.

I guess I was ready, or he was just tired of circling the block, because there, barreling down the night-thick street, was my zombie ride, its approaching taxi light like a weak and stumbling meteor weaving by and roaring past the brighter stars of approaching headlights.

A moment of hesitation as he pulled up next to me, my hand on the cold steel handle, but not opening it just yet. *You can do this, you can do this, you can do this.* Where first? What would Pogue do? Answer then, in his thunder and spit-raining blasts of fury: "Get off the fucking stick, you asshole-sucking excuse for a fucking vampire! When you don't know shit—which you fucking clearly do not—you find another asshole who does. Get off your fucking ass and get going."

Right, boss; sure, boss; whatever you say, boss. I didn't know Jack from Jack Shit, so I had to fill in the gaps, knock on some doors, and ask some questions. I had to do what I was paid blood to do. I had to do my job. Or at least try.

I had to go to the morgue. I just hoped I could get in without a reservation.

V

Over the hills and through the streets, up and over—a moment of air time there—we made our way. Outside I was the same Valentino I'd woken up as, minus perhaps a few pounds sweated out, plus a few hairs on my previously smooth chin, but inside I was doing *Le Corps Policier Contre* pushups, arm curls, lifts, squats, and stretches. *You are a cop (albeit a bright green one), you are a cop (trainee), you are a cop (without a clue), you are a cop (who doesn't know a thing), you are a cop (this is going to be so fucked up), you are a cop.*

You are here. "Here" doesn't look like much: just a steel door in a cement brick wall in the industrial and snotty loft zone of SOMA (South of Market to everyone else). The bottom part of an upper part of city buildings. Parking lot in front of said door more than half-full of cars. Standing in front of said door, in front of said cars, the usual doorman of the establishment: all tux and muscles, deep/dark shades, face as pale as the lifeless eyes of my driver, who pulled up in front. Name not known, just a fixture that came out when the sun went down.

To me, not a word, which was something that gladdened (a bit) my unbeating heart. Just a white, meaty hand to the door, and a back-handed knock. Either it was a slow night at the morgue and they needed to fill some seats, or having tagged along with Pogue all those other nights had given me a taste, a whiff, a tiny sprinkle of the fairy dust of authority.

Tall and straight, I made for the door. See Dick Powell walk, see Bogart saunter, see Powers Boothe stride, see Bruce Willis swagger.

See Valentino come up short.

Eyebrows beneath the sunglasses rising in re-estimation, the hand coming up, sausages in a patty of pallid meat, the mouth opened,

The Very Bloody Marys

doi:10.1300/5329_05

showing pearly whites too white to be real, and his voice grumbled and rumbled out at me: "Deliveries in back."

See Dick Powell stumble, see Bogart trip, see Powers Boothe hesitate, see Bruce Willis deflate. See Valentino stutter: "I-I'm here on business, official business."

"Hurm" was the sound he made, shades tilting down, then up. I felt rather than heard what he meant, knew in a second he'd add to that grumbly, growling sound of dismissal "Take a hike, kid," or a phrase of that general nature.

But I had a job to do. "Open the door, Tiny," I said, hoping my own tones were something that Dick Powell, Bogart, Powers Boothe, Bruce Willis would be proud of. But, to be honest, I doubt that even Rocky the Flying Squirrel would have quaked in his size-two moccasins at the sound of my voice.

I told you about the bad stuff, right? The beasties and nasties and creepies and shivers and shakes and quivers and quakes? Well, they exist and so, naturally, I guessed there had to be a flip side, right? A glowing and bright and happy and cheerful side to things. Didn't believe, not really, but then the doorman didn't say "Take a hike, kid," but rather, instead, grinned wide enough to show those fake pearlies and said, "Sure thing."

The door opened and I walked. Then, as the door closed behind me, he said, "Tell Pogue 'hello' for me, will ya?"

* * *

"Table for one?" Again with the up and the down of the eyes, bare this time, not hidden behind dark plastic lenses. The maître d' was in fine reds, a tux as crimson as the doorman's was black. Under his arm were gold-corded menus.

"I'm here on business. I need to speak with The Chef."

"The Chef? He is a very busy man, I'm afraid. I sincerely doubt that he would have a moment to spare to speak to . . . someone such as yourself. I do hope you'll understand."

"Just tell him it's official business. Tell him it's Valentino . . . and Pogue."

"I will do that. But please take a table. It does not look . . . proper . . . for you to simply wait here by the door. I do hope you'll understand."

Nodding, I was led past the gurneys, past the stainless-steel shelves, past rows of blue glass bottles and BIOHAZARD-stickered drums, past the filing drawers of the dead, past desks with green felt blotters, past darkened computer screens, past filing cabinets, past worktables fitted with drains, all under flickering fluorescent lights, and over white tile floors.

Naturally I got a table in the back, back against the drawers of the dead, next to a desk piled high with manila folders. The table, at least, was a neat little white-linened circle. Atop it were a votive candle with gently waving flame in a crystal holder, a tightly budded rose in a matching vase the color of a fine year of O positive, and finely filigreed silverware.

Snapping out the napkin, straightening my neck, I pretended that this was a place where I could afford to eat. Greetings, fellow diners. What wonderful weather we seem to be having!

"Good evening. Would sir like to hear the specials?"

My waiter for the evening was a classical, old-school ghoul. Don't get me wrong: some of my best friends are ghouls. I have nothing against them, not at all. After all, if someone decides they prefer the . . . company . . . of the living-disabled, what gives me the right to say that's a bad thing? To each his or her own, I say. Live and let. . . . Well, anyway, he was a ghoul, and despite myself my skin didn't just crawl, it got up and spoke its first words. If I'd have let it, it would have also walked out the door with the rest of me right behind it.

"Um, er—sure," I mumbled, trying to focus on anything but the color of his skin (slick and glossy seasick green in some places, mysterious continents of furry mold in others, broken up here and there with gleaming streaks of blacker corruption), the shape of his eyes (liquid sacks of yellow pus, wrinkles like fat spider webs radiating out from pupils swimming with restless maggots), or the architecture of his nose (about to drop off, it seemed, precariously resisting only by the power of a few less-diseased strands of cartilage).

"We have an excellent *veal al'anglaise,* which is served with salad nicoise. The veal is very fresh, collected only a few hours ago. We have a superb *ears a la hongroise,* which is accompanied by a fresh fruit salad. The ears are immaculate and free of any piercings, which, as sir most likely knows, can affect the flavor. We also are featuring a quite wonderful *escalopes foie gras cambacérès*; the liver from which it has been prepared has been marinating in an impertinent forty-proof liqueur for the past thirty years."

"I'm actually here just to speak to The Chef," I said before I lost what little appetite I had left. "Just a glass of your most affordable red would be fine."

"We have a . . . decent Chateu de Humbolt. Collected fresh this morning, the source having been vegetarian, it has the cloying aroma of nuts with just the slightest hints of fresh berries. It's only twenty dollars a glass."

"On second thought, just water."

"Water it is . . . sir," he said, nose pulled as high up as it could be, which wasn't that high as it really did look just about to fall off—landing, if there was any justice in this universe, in some unfortunate diner's consommé.

While waiting for my *vintage de la tap,* I scanned the gourmets in the back room, the few unfortunates who didn't have the clout for better tables.

Across from me, nestled between another desk and a brilliantly reflective row of sinks, was a dapper little incubus, all pretty smiles and perfectly tossed hair. Even off-duty, he seemed to be radiating an aura of availability and delicious promise. Alas, I was on duty, for one, and, for two, I didn't have enough to pay him to tell me the time.

A sigh then—a little, soft one to myself. Immortality—with or without a tan—is supposed to be time enough for anything, but so far the only sounds I could make were to myself. Just Valentino, only Valentino, forever. I know, I know: still time, still plenty of opportunities, but, I'll tell you, it's hard enough to spend a few months without a date, but quite another to spend a few decades. That amount of time can put a damper on even the most chirpy of optimists.

Okay, kid; time to get focused. Romance—or lack of it—later. You're here with a job to do, so get to it. I thought for a second about approaching the other diners to see if I could scare up a few leads, but aside from the incubus they looked like they were the ones to do the scaring, and had a lot more teeth than even I did. Aside from getting cold feet from their steely smiles, I didn't want to piss in The Chef's soup, what with him being one of our best sources of really underground, freshly killed and recently buried, or just-put-on-the-menu, leads.

"Sir?" asked my waiter, returning with a carafe of *eau de tap,* "The Chef says that he will see you now."

* * *

"Mr. Valentino, always a pleasure to see you. Sorry if I don't offer to shake hands, but this fellow's brain is rather slippery, as well as most likely wonderfully tasty, and I would simply hate to lose it."

"I . . . understand," I said, breathing deep and slow through my mouth. I probably looked like a grouper doing a lot of unnecessary and rather forced gaping. "I won't take too much of your time."

"No bother at all! I always enjoy a good chat with the various members of law enforcement. As you know, I pride myself on being a good and upstanding member of the community." With a sound that I never, ever want to hear again, The Chef tugged the brain free. The owner, laying face up on a steel gurney, didn't seem to mind much, his expression before The Chef's hands went into his sliced-open cranium staying exactly the same as when the five pounds of previous thoughts and memories came out. (This was a very neat trick, for anyone without a row of evenly placed bullet holes in his chest.) "Ah, I shall have to inform my select clientele that we shall have *cervelle* tonight. Maybe gently braised, Mr. Valentino? Or perhaps grilled with some onions? What is your favorite preparation?"

"Grilled . . . is . . . nice," I said, groveling even more. "Like I said, I don't want to keep you from your . . . chef thing, but I just wanted to hear whether you've heard anything."

"Being that I have a great many ears? Well, they are the special tonight," he said, putting an extra one next to his own, the owner still not minding one bit.

"Something like that, yes," I said, turning away from his flashing knives and overeager smile. Unlike his nighttime staff, The Chef could work on a tan; though, by his pallor, he clearly didn't. Also unlike his staff, and myself and Pogue, he was one of the few people, things, entities, creatures, beings, monsters, who could, and did, hold a nine (a.m.) to five (p.m.) job (though I heard he'd had to be extra careful when someone spied him eyeing a fresh bit of road kill with a culinary, rather than forensic, eye). "Have you heard about a group of loose cannon camps calling themselves the Very Blood Marys?"

"Ha ha!" he belly-rumbled as he slid a knife under the skin of the corpse, neatly slicing away a sliver of fatty flesh. "Kids these days. Have to give them a point or two for originality, though."

"Then you *have* heard of them?"

"Not a word, I'm afraid. Sorry to disappoint." The meat went into a polished kidney bowel with a faint *slap* of wetness. "If you don't mind me saying so, I couldn't help but notice that you seem to be alone. At first I thought that your brusque Mr. Pogue had stepped into the lavatory or something similar, but I do believe that I am entertaining only Mr. Valentino tonight, correct?"

"Which is my other question. My partner—"

"You mean your boss, if I may be impertinent."

"My boss, yes. He's gone missing. Hasn't been seen by anyone, including me, for days. Has he been by?" Trying to keep my cool, I'd strolled to one of the benches along the white tiled walls. Neatly arranged, by size or number of teeth, were various implements, knives next to knives, probes next to ladles, retractors next to graters, forceps next to skewers—row by row, one after another. Without thinking that it was used for both autopsy as well as that evening's special, I picked up a sinister-looking one.

"Well, this is a situation then, you being on your own. I doubt that the *Conseil* will be forthcoming with any additional resources, unless of course something were to go most terribly wrong. Do you think you can handle the responsibility, Mr. Valentino?"

"I think so." I hope so. "Pogue trained me very well." Not at all. "And I have contacts like yourself." Who, like your slippery self, probably won't give me the time of day.

"An admirable attitude. Well, as one of your so-called contacts, I hope you will use me as you see fit. After all, as I said, I do try to maintain a degree of decorum and professionalism with the various members of authority with whom it is my pleasure to deal—both in the daylight as well as at night."

The Chef was bald as an egg, smooth and pale as the flesh on the table in front of him. The only hint of any previous hair on his dome was a pair of caterpillars that looked about to mate above a pair of eyes the color and depth of gun barrels. Pogue didn't tell me a lot, but I remember the one time, just before we approached the doorman, he'd turned to me and said, in as much of a whisper as his machine-gun-and-artillery-fire voice could muster: "This fucking asshole'd cut off, cook up, and serve his goddamned dick if he thought he'd get something out of it." Noted, but I sure as hell didn't want to wait around for that prep, cook, and serve.

"Gotcha. So I take it that, as a fine and upstanding member of society, you haven't seen my boss around?"

"Alas, Mr. Valentino, while I wish I could say I have, I cannot. Last time I saw Mr. Pogue was when he was here last, with you. But perhaps I might be of service in some other way?"

"Oh?" I said, returning the knife to its row of kin, but more than a bit askew, even a tad sloppily. Take that, asshole! "Any cooperation would be gratefully appreciated," I said, as coldly as I could deliver.

"While I may not be able to help with your search for either the wittily named 'Marys,' or even to locate your missing employer, I am not without my facilities, both as coroner as well as The Chef of this humble establishment. In either capacity, I will note anything unusual that might come to my attention. But beyond my intelligence-gathering ability, might I also offer you something else?"

"And what would that be?"

"You seem to be a bit on the thin side, Mr.Valentino. Might I offer you a few morsels to take with you in your noble pursuits? A 'doggy bag' to show my appreciation for your services to the community as our liaison to *Le Conseil Carmin*. Please, take it."

I did. Stupid, I know; you don't have to remind me. God knows, for the next few days I did enough reminding of myself. So, with my brown paper gift he pulled from a short row of neatly stapled row of same off to the side, I tapped my eyebrow (no way in heaven or hell or all points between was I going to shake those hands) and went out into the dining area and then out into the parking lot, the alabaster face of the doorman cracking neither a smile nor a frown as I stepped out.

On the street, no sign of Mariah, which meant that either I had business of some kind left to do or zombies had a lunch break. Knowing they didn't, I ran through my mind my visit with the tasty dead, and came up short. Not exactly a fortuitous visit or start of my investigation that my undead cabbie knew more than I did.

It was only then that I popped open the bag and looked in. *Okay,* I thought, dropping it into the sewer for the one or two things lower and dumber than myself to enjoy: *Message received, and noted.*

As Mariah pulled up and I got in to head off to my next possible lead, I looked quickly back at the door and the doorman, and thought about The Chef, the presenter of a brown paper bag of dozens of fresh and still-moist human eyeballs: *I'm going to keep my eyes on you, too.*

VI

Rising (whee!) and falling (ouch!) with the crest and descent of the city's well-known manic-depressive geography, the faded and split upholstery squeaking, squeaking, squeaking with failing springs each time, Mariah piloting, me hanging on for dear life, we headed away from downtown and out toward the fog belt. For the daylight people, the regular folks, the Sunset and Richmond districts were two sides of the same coin, separated by the green of Golden Gate Park. For the nighttime people, the irregular folks—the shadows, the shades, the spooks—Sunset and Richmond were the hesitant lands, the transforming acres, tentative real estate. Places where this could be that, and that might even be this.

The fog that slipped between the row houses, that blurred the edges of Doegler's repetitive architecture, spinning and twisting among the alphabetically named avenues, made more than concrete and brick driveways and bay windows vague and uncertain. The white rolling, the ghostly churning similarly pushed the already permeable barrier to its limit. Was that a Plywood Specialty Woodnymph (paneled skin and knotty eyes) coming out of that Chinese market? Could that have been the Sacred Locomotive of Kioram taking the place of the N Judah light rail vehicle (gleaming gold, flashing diamond, and deeply lustrous plutonium)? Might that have been a Lantern of Aristophanes regally perambulating across an intersection (shimmering silks and opulent velvets trailing behind like ornate smoke)? Could be, might be, perhaps, maybe, possibly . . .

I hated it. Bad enough to prowl the halls and corridors of downtown, where the shadows nipped at your ankles and—according to Pogue—Things That Shouldn't Be Named looked at you with sly schemings and horrible ponderings. They think with minds of maggots and icky corruption, *Would his soul be good straight or on a nice point*

The Very Bloody Marys

doi:10.1300/5329_06

of perfectly browned toast? But back there, at least the map didn't change from block to block. As bad as they were, things stayed where they were. Out on the Avenues though, the definitions were way too slick, too hesitant, too damned foggy.

If I had my way, I'd never cross the city, not set a damned undead moccasin in this part of San Francisco. Not even for Saul—and of all the people, beings, creatures, monsters, and things Pogue and I dealt with, Saul was one of the few I actually liked. But I didn't have my way, didn't have Pogue, and so I had to cross the city, putting not one but both of my size tens in this domain of vague definitions, hazy doorways, fuzzy perceptions, and indistinct horrors.

Then, we were there. For me, it was just a tooth in a mile-long smile of pale stucco. Another set of stairs up to another simple door. Another row of windows above a garage. It could have been any of a thousand houses in this part of the city. In fact, it was always a different house each time I came out here. Saul liked few things more than his security, and so shuffled his address with each and every dawn. And among the people, beings, creatures, monsters, and things Pogue and I dealt with, Saul could do it. Which is probably why he had to do it.

Out the door, for some reason I had a rise in my mood, a spring in my step, and so I tossed back at the unmoving (thank god) Mariah behind the wheel, "I shan't be a moment, Jeeves."

No answer. Never was. A flash memory of soulless eyes, face like an infielder's glove and, not for the first time, the last, or anything between, I was glad there wasn't.

Up the stairs, my hand on the knocker became a brass-on-brass clunk of sound as I announced myself. After a few seconds, the sound of remote thunder, a storm coming in from a long way away, then a steady, metronome earthquake that evolved into a precise series of explosions—all coming toward the door.

Below the knocker, a black-painted grill the size of a playing card, an ace of security, which suited Saul too well. Silence, the thunder, earthquakes, explosions halting. Then the grill opened.

"Hi, Abe," I said to the brass-cast face of Abraham Lincoln as it peered out at me. "I'm here to see the wizard."

* * *

The outside might change but the inside of Saul's place always stayed the same. Gloomy—like the deepest, murkiest pit in the deepest, murkiest part of the deepest, murkiest place you could imagine—and packed baseboard to rafters with books, books, books, books, and even more books, laid flat, spines sideways, totally obscuring what was potentially wallpaper. In the canyon between thick leather bindings and particularly arcane paperbacks, thick planks on top of thick panels nailed to even more thick timbers, bringing the rafters dangerously low for every inch the reinforced floorboards added.

Abe wasn't much of a conversationalist. Like Mariah, he probably knew a helluva lot, but while I hoped my driver would always stay silent (to avoid the image of those grisly lips parting, curious black-bodied spider weaving between yellowed tombstones of crooked corpse teeth, dust and webs exhaling with whatever words he wanted to speak), Abe *had to*: he had lips but nothing behind them.

Saul never said where he got Abe, but, looking at him, I had a suspicion that some dozy little burg in the heartland had woken one bright and way-too-cheerful morning to find its tiny weed-plagued park absent the rail-splitter's brass effigy. That loss became Saul's bodyguard and helpmate.

As he led the way, I kept from toppling over from each of his pounding steps by grabbing onto the firmest-looking stacks of ancient and forgotten lore. Finally, the Brass Ass of the Great Emancipator led me through silverfish heaven to a narrow doorway between the piles. Beyond was a tiny kitchen, just a sink and counter, fridge and stove, dingy but remaining warm and inviting. In it was Saul, tarnished silver hair, rainbow sweater unwinding in spots into primary colors, brittle bones showing where unwinding yarn couldn't hide it, eyes like bleached robin's eggs, Indian blanket in his lap hiding the bones I knew weren't just brittle but also didn't work, and, because of those legs, an ancient wheelchair. In his lap, a portly marmalade tabby glowered up at me, inscrutable thoughts behind an obviously wicked expression as I stepped in.

"What is it that sucks as well as blows?" the cat asked, grinning a pointed smile.

"Again with the put-downs, Cheshire?" Saul said, shooing the feline critic from his lap. "I've told you and I've told you: give a little good, you get a little good. Maybe a fish. Maybe some milk. Use your claws, Mr. Nasty, and you sleep in the yard."

The feline critic landed with the sound of a pork chop slapping onto a plate. It slinked toward the door, tail and head too high, parting shot without even a head turn: "Feh. I just utter as I see, old man."

"Never mind him, Val. He's been a nasty little hairball ever since I cut down on his little problem. Right, Mr. I-don't-need-catnip-I-can-quit-whenever-I-want?" he yelled to the tight little asterisk of the cat's behind as it slipped out. When it completely had, he swung azure irises toward me and smiled, flipping his hands open and palms up. "So, Val, what is it this broken-down old man can do you for?"

* * *

The tea was good, warm, and sweet trickling down my throat. Because it was tea or because all I usually drank was blood and booze, I couldn't say. All I could tell, then and there, was it was good, so I sipped more.

"Gherkin," Saul said, sipping from his own cup. "That is, quite a pickle—as my Aunt Estelle would say. Bless her soul. One of my favorites, Estelle was. Best knish you ever tasted. She could help you find whatever it was you lost by rubbing the tip of your nose with a feather."

"You know the same trick, Saul?"

"I wish. Me? I burn water to a crisp. And Estelle, she took the rest of her tricks with her. Not that I don't have my own little ways. A bit of this, a bit of that. Not that I'm bragging or anything, but I do know a bit more than old Estelle."

"I appreciate it. I really do."

"Don't mention it. But I have to tell you, Val, I wouldn't worry about those ugly little biters. Sure, they might be ruining the neighborhood and all, but when you get right down to it, they're just a bunch of vamps. No insult, you know. Present company excluded."

"Right, Saul. I've got you."

"But Pogue, my boy—well, what can I say? Either the fellow is hiding out somewhere, which you or I don't really think is the case, or, heaven forbid, he's got himself in his own pickle. And a gherkin that would put *that* man out, well, meet him I would not want to."

Until then, that moment, I hadn't thought of that. Pogue was steel and brass, gunpowder and grit. Not a vamp anything or anyone could take down, or not without a fight that half the city—daylight or night—would notice. I guess in the back of my mind I'd seen him hiding out, all of this just another damned test for Valentino, another excuse to tear me a new one, or well-use the old one.

I never thought that anything would have happened to him, never suspected for a second that Pogue would have met his unearthly match. But sitting in the wizard's kitchen, golem Abe standing loyally in the doorway, I had to. It wasn't pleasant; the thought, that is, not Saul and his statue.

Steel and brass, gunpowder and grit. Tough as nails, mean as a snake, harder to kill than a cliché. So what could? The Sarge was still, as Saul put it, just a vamp, although a vamp that would rip off many a head and spit down many a neck.

The list wasn't a long one. But it was long enough to make me put my knees together and grip Saul's hefty coffee mug tightly. An inventory of terror flickered through and between my ears, page after page of things that slunk and struck, slobbered and howled, clawed and bit, oozed and infected, crawled and chewed, flew and spit, swam and digested, and hopped and screamed.

That was the list I knew of. Pogue—I said it before, and it's worth saying again—hadn't told me everything, not even close. My list wasn't long, but each page was still terrifying. Pogue's was at least twice as long . . . three times? Four? Five? It wasn't what I knew that lowered my temperature, but what I didn't.

Crap. Shit. Fuck.

"Shame our Mr. Pogue couldn't have one of those new cellular telephones," Saul said, sing-song voice chirping up into some cheerful octaves.

I was down quite a bit, at the bottom of a deep, dark well full of creepy, slithering things, so it took me a stretch of time to realize he was showing off to me. Saul, whose idea of "modern" was an electric stove, had mentioned something from this century. He must have pulled his gray hairs from the ancient bindings and sheaves to notice a bit of the outside world.

That made me smile, a grin to my frowning, stiff face. Not for long, though. Back in the early nineties, the gadgets had attracted the similarly old-world eyesight of the *Conseil* and an experiment had been made to outfit some of us with them. Shudder, shudder, and shudder again. Okay for a few nights—until the limbo-trapped ectoplasmic remains of a few hundred thousand Egyptian cats that'd been sacrificed had found our band on the broadcast spectrum. Endless hours of ghostly purrs, spectral vowels, and otherworldly screeches had landed Pogue and me in the trash, clanking and crashing with satisfaction. More perils of working the other side, more trials and further tribulations of living in the shadows at night.

A memory, fleet-footed and furtive: Pogue and I at the ass end of an alley near the Castro, bright lights of the big city at the far end of a dark urban canyon. The brass-assed sergeant and I jump-shooting the devices into the darkness, the cacophony of their hits bouncing back and forth in the narrow space. Perhaps it was the relief of getting rid of the damned things, or maybe impact's perfect little clanking and crashing chorus, possibly. I don't know, but we'd spontaneously laughed: kettle drum from Pogue, flutes from me.

Where the hell was he? What the fuck was going on?

"Thanks for the tea, Saul, but I'd better hit the bricks."

"Feh. No biggie, Val. Let me know if you hear anything from that old bastard. I know I'll be sleeping easier after he shows up."

Would I be? Laughter in an alley. . . . But, forgetting that, would I be better off without him? He was the boss, the Big Bad Man, the Cop of Cops—at least to me. He was the Thin Red (Blooded) Line Between THEM and US. . . . But, forgetting that (and it was very hard to), would I be better off without him? From what he'd told me, I was already lucky the Things That Slurped and Lurched and Ate Babies for Breakfast hadn't already feasted on my (relatively) young vampire hide.

But what about me? I'd been ordered by Ombre to get him back. The city needed him back. I needed him back. But did I *want* him back?

Out of the kitchen—honest and sincere nod of appreciation to Saul as I walked—the thunder, the storm, the earthquake, explosions behind me from there to the front door, Abe escorting me to the front door.

Out into the fog, a chill of more than atmosphere. Saul's address had changed again, the steps and neighborhood having shifted between sips of my tea. I walked out into unfamiliar territory, an unknown land.

Behind me, the door closing. But before it was completely shut: "Abe?" I said to the golem. The patina face of the presidential monument looked up at me with corroded eyes. "Take care of the old man, 'kay?"

Was that a nod? It could have been a nod. Whatever it was, it was short and quick because I was then alone on the steps, Abe back inside with the wizard.

Alone on the street, uncertain mists swirling down the avenue. Headlights coming close but then passing me by, fog sweeping around the passing metal box. No Mariah, not yet. Unfinished business, I wondered, or not knowing where to find me yet?

Business. . . . I hated Pogue. Yes, that was it, no question about it; if for no other reason than for being mean enough to hide from me or stupid enough to get himself killed. But I didn't have a choice. I had a job. I had orders.

So, out into a city I barely understood, to deal with puzzles with teeth, enigmas with poisonous venom, deadly rebuses, riddles with quivering spines, conundrums with glassy eyes. To find a bunch of rogue biters before they nibbled and drank their way through the precious blood supply of San Francisco. To find my boss, the Big Bad Man, the Cop of Cops—before I stepped where I shouldn't, walked into something I shouldn't, and got myself killed.

Headlights again, a smudge of yellow among the smoky white fog, going from the middle of the street to pulling up in front of me. My ride.

Love, hate; what I wanted, what I didn't want. In the end neither mattered: I had a job to do.

VII

Most working stiffs—none of them quite as stiff as my beloved Mariah, perhaps—commonly consider jobs to be nine to five. If they should happen to forget, the worst that can happen is that they stay late and make the boss happy, or get in late and create the opposite emotion in the fart who signs the paycheck.

Rising and falling over ribbons of asphalt, the slow stroboscopic beat of streetlights through the cab's windows, the sudden color splashes of STOP, SLOW, and GO breaking up the glaring monotony, I put my Italian nose to the cool glass and looked out at the city. Thoughts bubbled and popped in my head, popcorn fantasies, kernels of hope exploding then vanishing against my personal harsh reality.

Then, my eyes got wider, the city glow coming more and more into my pupils, because what dawned on me at that moment was that the city was glowing a bit more than the bright stars of streetlamps, the primary brilliance of stoplights, the blurred rainbows of signage, neon as well as cheaper fluorescents. It dawned on me, in fact, just what was rapidly approaching.

Dawn.

"Um, er, ah . . . Mariah?" Charm never hurt anyone, or so I hoped. "*Dear?* Maybe we should be heading back to my digs? Fast?" I looked again, saw again, that the sky was lightening, the black slipping away to a fast-approaching purple. "Very fast?"

If Mariah heard, he made no sign, of course. He made no sign at all—neon or fluorescent or any other kind—and instead did as he always did, only what he could do, and drove. But he drove neither faster nor slower than he had since we had left Saul's place in the hesitant mists of the Avenues.

"I really hate to be a backseat driver, but I'd really appreciate a bit of . . . acceleration," I said, clearing my throat to hopefully perk up his

The Very Bloody Marys

doi:10.1300/5329_07

gnarled mushroom ears, "since it's getting to be that time when all the good bloodsuckers should be hiding from the sun."

Wheels spinning, tires doing their tractioning best, we careened through the city. Did we just blast through a yellow? Did we just tear through a red? Did we graze that baby carriage? Did we just knock over that old woman? Did we just scrape against that bus?

Was the sky getting brighter?

The answer to the only question I really cared about was a positive, absolute, definite YES as I twisted my neck around to look back and up where the stars were now gone and that deep velvety purple was now a positive golden sweep of sunrise. Shadows. There were actual shadows then, the night retreating to its usual hiding places, sliding up against the sides of buildings, swinging around to skulk in alleyways, retreating to holes and doorways.

A landmark. Fuck yes, that was what I thought it was: the loops of unlit neon, a sign of home, a sign of safety. Twin Peaks, the bar, meant that The Midnight Sun, below my home, was just around the corner.

Then we were around that corner, Mariah's squealing tires pushed beyond their grip on the road, and we were there. I was home.

Hand beating, clawing, madly clutching the door handle and then OUT, across the pale seam of the sidewalk and up against my heavy door. Keys. God, so many of the damned things. The brass one. That one. That's it. In—upside down! Damn! There, got it, turn, turn, turn, push and—

Cool. Dark. Safe. Whew. Breathe in, breathe out. Nothing burning, nothing smoking. Just a dusty smell, a hallway smell, a safe and home smell.

Up the flight, still breathing heavily, fear tapping a clenched fist in my rib cage, the beat fading steadily as the cool safety of home seeped into my clammy skin.

Up the flight, and then breathing even heavier, heart hammering a hummingbird tempo when I realized that I wasn't alone in the cool comfort of my apartment.

Because sitting there on the edge of my unmade bed was Julian.

* * *

Oh oh oh Julian Julian Julian—beloved, adored, venerated companion, compadre, mate, playmate, partner, betrothed, idol, best friend, love, lover—oh oh oh Julian Julian Julian. . . .

Julian: hand in mine, lips on mine, other body parts on mine. Eyes of cobalt ice set in a perfect anatomical setting of glacial white. Hair Aztec gold, Tiffany brilliant, Fort Knox, 14 carat, sure, shiny, gleaming blond. Nose regal, princely, Roman (not hawk, hooked, or at all goombah), elegant, eloquent, slender, and shapely. Lips lush, lips full, lips silk, lips tender, lips strong, lips pert, lips bowed, lips sweet, lips—oh lips oh lips. Cheeks high and dancing with laughter and tight with joy. A body of marble, muscles of corded iron and bundled steel, perks defined with hard lines as ideal nouns of certain and spectacular formation and well-cut form. Legs columnar, thighs forged by honest work and resolute exercise, knees like dimpled ideals. Calves of skin-and-bone poetry, stanzas of structure. Well-turned ankles. Feet concluding with the precious xylophone notes of cutesy-wootsy toes dancing under the covers that would then be stringed instruments sliding under silk sheets. Arms to carry, arms to hold, arms to flex, arms to lift, arms to protect, arms to wrap, arms to never let go, arms to embrace, arms to hug, arms to cuddle, arms to squeeze, arms to grasp, arms to welcome, arms never to hit, never to push, never to release, never to slap, never to drop—never, ever to let go. Hands of dexterity and grace, elegance and refinement, art and wit, kindness and skill, tickles and music—lightly tapped keys or a carefully held bow—applause and perfectly executed grips and pulls and strokes and touches.

Julian of the ages, Julian of times and times again. Julian who has always been here and will always be here. Julian when I was twelve, darting and running and laughing and screaming with cobblestones under our feet, tents, stalls, Roman walls, marble stairs and ghostly plastered houses flashing by our childish eyes. Julian when I was twenty, us on the side of a hill, a carpet of grass beneath us, a pure cerulean sky too high above, the baking radiation of a summer sun interrupted only by amiably ambling clouds.

Julian when I was seventy, sharing glasses of a fine hemotype while he celebrated me with gloriously ravishing praise for my accomplishments as a man, as a vamp, as an officer in high and good standing with the *Conseil.* Julian when I was one hundred, having had enough of Pogue and his constant, incessant diminishing of me, rolling up his fine silken sleeves and neatly—with a few blindingly fast lefts and amazingly quick rights—kicking my boss's ass.

Julian, sitting on the edge of my bed, right now. Here, this minute, this moment, this instant, with me.

Julian of laughter and joy, Julian of hope and love. Julian of delight and arousal. Julian who makes me feel special. Julian who says I deserve to be, and am, loved. Julian who says I deserve to be, and am, respected and admired. Julian who says I should be, and am, cherished.

Julian, who holds me close and tight and whispers endearments and sweetness into my ears. Julian, who rubs my feet when they ache. Julian, who holds my hands when we walk down the bright and sunny streets of every town I have ever lived in or have ever wanted to live in. Julian, who lays his coat down on rainy gutters so that my delicate feet may never touch mud. Julian, who leaves roses for me to find. Julian, who puts chocolates on my pillow. Julian, who hugs me close and kisses my cheek amid cinema flickers and flashes of fictitious romance on the silver screen. Julian, who tousles my hair. Julian, who pinches my ass. Julian, who touches my lips with a quivering finger, saying as he does: "I can't believe you're real."

That time in Venice, the canals smelling of roses and sweet wine. He and I, hand in hand, walking the arcing bridges, watching the sun rise over filigreed balustrades, morning glow sweeping over the brilliance of windows and the fireworks of fresh flowers in window boxes. Mozart in the air, the tunes of joy and happiness spilling—no, *shared*—from one of those windows, a performance for us and our steps in that ancient city. Julian and I, in Venice, and he turns to me and says it. The words that others have said but never meant, the words that mean what he says, and only what he means.

That time in Paris, sitting in the descending afternoon, the imminent dusk, sipping thick coffees, dusting our lips with the powdered sugar from puff pastry. A slow and easy day in the City of Lights. Walks and merry chatter. The exact subjects forgotten, the precise route not remembered. Just that city, that day, in a café. A spoon at the tips of my fingers, straightening it, aligning silver with a seam in the tablecloth. Bringing unnecessary order to a place of spiral and twisting avenues and boulevards. A silly and common gesture. Then, the knowledge—certain and pure—that he was looking at me. Really looking at me—and seeing me. I lifted my head from my alignment to witness his vision. Then he said those three words, and the tears immediately started their run down my face.

That time in New York. The war was over. The war was finally over. The boys wouldn't die anymore. We were in Times Square when the news came, blaring from radios, screamed from relieved throats. Over, finally over. He, I remember, was in his uniform, all starch and precision, all snap and attention. I was in a lovely suit, precision but of a different order. Elegant (me) and proper (him) in Times Square as the world cried and screamed and laughed and tossed their hats into the air. Then I was in his arms, being dipped back. Then his lips were on mine and there was a kiss—no, an error, a mistake. It was *the* kiss, the one all others descended from. In Times Square, at the end of the war. Then the kiss was in the past, and he was saying to me those three words.

That time on the beach. Sand between our toes, sand between our cheeks, suits wads of synthetics in less than dignified piles next to us, their colors barely touching the towels we sprawled on. The sun above, baking us golden brown, simmering the oils that coated our fine, streamlined bodies. Any conversation hushed by the waves, suppressed by the aroma of hot salt from both the sea and our sweat. Too hot to touch. Too hot to move. But then he did, rolling over onto his side, one nipple appearing, the other vanishing as his chest twisted. His face, then, next to mine, and he said something. A phrase beginning lovely and ending beautiful. The start: "I don't want to be anywhere but here, with you." The ending: three words that pushed me beyond being on the hot sand, under a hot sun, and into his arms.

Julian, sitting on the edge of my bed. How long did I stand there and look at him? How many minutes, how many hours? How many years? Then Julian, who sat on the edge of my bed, a vision, a delight, a wonder, a dream, smiled, and the curtain of his tight and so-soft lips parted to show me teeth the brightness and brilliance of absolute alabaster, with two of the sexiest and cutest little sharp and ever-soslightly elongated incisors, and he said, in words like bells or the most beautiful musician playing on the most fantastic instrument that ever existed: "I could do with a bite. You up for Chinese food?"

"Chinese? Right! Chinese? Absolutely! Chinese? Sure! Chinese? Positively! Chinese? What a wonderful suggestion! You wait right here. So sorry about the mess. Ohmygod, it's so great to see you, you look fabulous and sexy and amazing and incredible and . . . did I mention sexy? Because if I didn't then I should and if I did I really should say it again because of how sexy you look, which is like, a lot. A real lot. Chinese? Oh, right, Chinese. Chinese it is. I know of a great place and I think you'll really like it and if you don't really like it I'll go anywhere because it's so great to see you and I've missed you so much and a second, a minute, an hour, a day, a month, a year, a decade, a century hasn't gone by that I haven't thought about and missed you so much but now you're back and it's so wonderful I can barely contain myself and you're looking really good and by that I mean not just good because lots of things can be good like Chinese food (ha ha ha ha) but you look a lot better than just egg noodles and sprouts or tofu or sweet-and-sour anything. I mean, look at me, I can't think straight but then that's me, like you said I couldn't ever think straight but it's just because you're here and it's fantastic . . . no, incredible . . . I don't have the words, I just don't have the words."

Then Julian, who was still sitting on the edge of the bed, said those three words: "I am hungry."

And I whipped around, bolted down the stairs, hit the door, and was out into a fresh night. In search of Chinese food, because Julian, my beloved, wonderful, fantastic, magical, Julian was sitting on the edge of my bed, and was hungry.

* * *

How many minutes had I stood there and looked at him? How many minutes, how many hours? Luckily for me it was hours, and not just minutes, because it *was* a fresh night I ran into and not a warm, sunny day. But even if the sun had been up and I'd taken up smoking again—from every square inch of skin—I would have done anything to get out, go down the street, and pick up some nice sweet, some good sour for my beloved Julian.

But, as I said, luck was with me because Julian was waiting for me and it wasn't broad and mean-ass daylight outside and so I didn't burst into flame and do an impression of a well-used ashtray. So, out. Running like I'd never run before. Sprinting through the guys, gals, and various combinations and betweens of a night in the Castro, a mad sprint in pursuit of Chinese, because Julian was waiting for me back in my apartment.

Was that Mariah, idling there on the corner? No matter. Nothing mattered. Not Pogue. Not the Bloody Marys. Not anything but feet to pavement, running, running, running up 18th Street to Castro proper, then eyes right, up the hill, and eyes right, up another hill (my neighborhood at the bottom of both but also up another one; welcome to San Francisco), looking for Chinese chow. Nothing, nothing, nothing. Panic, then, standing there on the corner. Back to my place, to tell the delightful love of my life that I would just be a few more minutes while I hunted down food worthy of his perfection? It would mean being with him again. It would mean seeing him sitting there on the edge of my bed and being able to gaze into his delightful countenance. It would mean those eyes, that nose, those lips. . . .

Then, up one of the hills (no, I won't say which one, smartass), a sign not in English, and so meaning Chinese. Logic! Brilliance! Across the street, skipping through the headlight glare of nighttime traffic and down the sidewalk, weaving then not through honking horns and shrieking brakes and skidding tires but rather past shrieking queens and skidding muscle boys. None of them as pretty or as buffed as my Julian, who was sitting on the edge of my bed, back in my apartment, waiting for Chinese food.

In the door, past the tables, up to the register. "To go!" at the little guy behind it, who jumped back in shock at the sight of me (were my teeth showing?), collecting himself just enough to thrust a two-fold menu at me.

Julian was waiting for me. Julian was waiting for Chinese food. Julian sitting on the edge of my unmade bed, waiting for Chinese food. Julian of the cobalt eyes, the perfection of nose, the elegance of form, the wonder of smile, my dream, my love—and I didn't know what the hell I was looking at. See, the problem of being on a liquid diet for too long is that neon and plastic signs saying things like PIZZA, BURGERS, SUSHI, SUBS, DELI, BISTRO, BAKERY, GROCERY, GYROS, McDONALD'S, JACK IN THE BOX, WENDY'S, BURGER KING, DOMINO'S, and BBQ are just letters on glowing signs. I knew some of it, of course, from the days before I sipped cheap, common blood in shots, but none of it prepared me for that menu, that day, with Julian waiting.

Exasperated, frustrated, wild-eyed, desperate, manic, panicked, I flipped the menu around to face the wide eyes of the manager and stabbed a quivering finger at something from column A, column B, and column C. That seemed to do the trick, or at least he didn't laugh at me.

How long did I wait? How many minutes, hours, days, weeks, years did I sit in a chair by the register, folding, unfolding, folding, unfolding, folding, unfolding, folding the menu until it was the size of a matchbook? I don't know, but it was a lot of some of them and probably only a few of the others. But it sure felt like a lot of the big ones before a white plastic bag was produced with three plastic-coated, cardboard boxes inside. Money was exchanged, and I barely minded the thought of the money being spent on my prince, my wonder, my delight, my light, my love, before I grabbed the bag and tore out the door.

The street, the corner, the traffic, the honks, the profanity, the pedestrians, the profanity, my door, my lock, my key, my shoulder, my stairs, my feet, my voice: "Honey! I'm home!"

My God.

Because sitting there on the edge of my unmade bed was Julian.

Not pretty, not handsome, not sexy, not beautiful, not a vision, not a treasure. Julian, on the edge of my bed, wrinkles and decay, dust and corruption. Gray and ancient, stooped and twisted. Cataracts and liver spots. Missing teeth and sagging skin.

Then he said something—a few wheezing, gasping words—and died.

VIII

WHY IS OUR BEER THE BEST? WHY IS OUR FURNITURE SO INEXPENSIVE? WHY IS OUR FINANCING SO REASONABLE? WHY IS OUR TONIC SO HEALTHY? WHY DO WE HAVE SO MANY BOOKS? WHY DO WE HAVE THE BEST PRODUCE? WHY ARE OUR PIANOS SO EXCELLENTLY CRAFTED? WHY ARE OUR RADIOS SO AFFORDABLE? WHY IS OUR CARPETING SUPERIOR? WHY DO WE HAVE MORE SHEET MUSIC THAN ANYONE ELSE? WHY DO WE HAVE SO MUCH EXCELLENT CABINETRY? WHY DO WE HAVE THE MOST STATIONERY STUFF? WHY ARE OUR BUGGIES AND CARRIAGES OF SUCH HIGH QUALITY? WHY DO WE HAVE THOUSANDS OF RUGS? WHY ARE WE THE PLACE FOR DRUGS? WHY SHOULD LADIES BUY DRESSES FROM US? WHY DO WE HAVE SUCH A HUGE AND CRYPTIC SIGN?

Ten thousand questions in the naked city. These are but seventeen of them.

Two stories at least, announced in a simple but stylish font. Glowing green and white at night, a puzzle to residents and voyeurs alike, the sign was a cryptic illumination over the busy intersection: Who made it? What were those reasons? And why were there only seventeen of them? People had sought the answers for a long time, and if you're looking for an explanation here . . . well, you won't find it.

WHY DOES THE MOON STAY IN THE SKY? WHY DO CLOUDS GO AWAY? WHY DOES THE EARTH TURN BENEATH OUR FEET? WHY IS THE SKY BLUE? WHY DOES THE SUN BURN? WHY CAN'T WE SEE AIR? WHY DOES THE WIND HOWL? WHY DOES RAIN COME IN DROPS? WHY IS SNOW HEAVY? WHY DOES THUNDER FOLLOW LIGHTNING? WHY DOES LIGHTNING COME BEFORE THUNDER? WHY DOES NIGHT CHASE THE DAY? WHY DOES THE DAY FOLLOW NIGHT? WHY DOESN'T ANYONE DO ANYTHING ABOUT THE WEATHER? WHY IS THE

The Very Bloody Marys

doi:10.1300/5329_08

COLDEST WINTER A SUMMER IN SAN FRANCISCO? WHY DOES PAIN STAY? WHY DOES JOY LEAVE?

I had a revelation on the corner of 17th and Mission—though it had nothing to do with "17 Reasons." Standing there in the warm blanket of a summer night, traffic blurring past with only the occasional thumping bass accompaniment from some "turned-up-way-too-high" stereo, I looked at a door I'd never seen before, and thought: *ugliness has its own kind of invisibility.*

A fat brown log of shit, more disgusting for its obvious humanity; a pick-up-stick pile of cheap needles, one of their tips still red-crusted; a glazed pool of urine, the door eroded where it had been splashed by countless generations of drunks, metal plate holed by the acid of poorly digested beer. Even the door itself, where it was whole, was repulsive: decades of graffiti, gang tags, commands to "FUCK YOU" in a dozen languages covered its dull metal surface. If it had an original color, it was long since buried under spray-painted hate, profanity, and feral territory markings.

Why did Julian have to die? Why did Julian have to die? Why did Julian have to die? Why did Julian have to die? Why did Julian have to die? Why did Julian have to die? Why did Julian have to die? Why did Julian have to die? Why did Julian have to die? Why did Julian have to die? Why did Julian have to die? Why did Julian have to die? Why did Julian have to die? Why did Julian have to die? Why did Julian have to die? Why did Julian have to die? Why did Julian have to die?

It was a perfect hiding place. After all, a door could always be opened. The trick was to make one that no one *wanted* to open.

Blessing my sneakers, I reached out for the knob, feeling the soles skate and squish beneath me. As if standing at the brink, I mumbled the mantra "just don't look down" as I turned and pushed.

* * *

Stairs ascending. Where, I didn't know. Heaven or hell, I didn't care.

I started up, one shit-covered shoe in front of the other.

Hollow, cored. Empty, burned up. There was something else though, a single resident in the wreck of what-I-used-to-be, a new resident peering out through the smashed windows of my eyes, a tenant in the attic of my mind. He may have looked like me, sounded like me, moved like me, but he was new—someone born just a few minutes ago, brought screaming and crying into the world only recently.

When I held the decaying remains of Julian in my arms.

People might have seen him as he walked out of my apartment. They may have nodded and waved, thinking he was the old Valentino, the one he resembled so closely. They may even have spoken to him, wishing him a good night, asking how he was, or simply just nodding.

But that had not been Valentino stepping out into the street, turning and moving down 18th Street toward the salsa and graffiti of the Mission District. Appearances would have been completely deceiving.

Valentino was dead.

I was what was left.

* * *

At the top, another door. This one not invisible. This one asking to be opened. Hand out, I did what I hadn't done before and looked down. Not sitting completely in the frame, there was a gap at the bottom. As I glanced down, I saw light spilling out. A bright light. Not a natural light.

I didn't care. Julian's ashes were still on my hands. Palms on the knob, I could feel the last of him—gritty and faintly scratching my skin against the polished metal. Just before his last breath, moments before his heart stopped beating and his eyes slowly closed, his mouth had opened, a decaying and corrupted maw, and he'd spoken.

Two words. No, a number and a word. Meaning a location: "17 Reasons."

He'd wanted me to come here.

That was enough for me.

* * *

The Boy was illuminated.

Such light shouldn't have existed, but it did: a glow beyond anything I knew, anything in my experience. I stood on an immaculately polished floor, the sparkling spires of the nighttime city beyond, silk drapes rippling in a barely felt breeze, and was speechless. The quiet was not just a negative from my lips; rather, the silence was deep, penetrating—a quiet trench in my mind. My soul was hushed.

"Hello," The Boy said. Bells, chimes, wind through ancient trees. A sound that couldn't be reproduced, couldn't be defined; any attempt was inaccurate at best, blasphemous at worst.

"Uh . . . hi," I said, trying not to think about the shit on my shoes, the rip in my very unwashed jeans, the stink emanating from my rancid pits under my old and grimy T-shirt. The stubble on my face; my unwashed and greasy hair, halitosis, the zits on my back, the crescents of grime under my ragged fingernails . . .

"Thank you for coming," The Boy said, voice seeming to drop an octave or two, as if descending a staircase. At the top, the gleaming of angel wings; at the bottom, a smelly basement.

"I–I had to come," I said, breaking away from The Boy's stare to look around the room.

"I understand," The Boy said, and through his tone and words, I knew he really did.

"H-he asked me. He was th-there. I was holding him. In my arms. And he said . . . he said. Oh, God." Tears again, hot and fast, racing down my face. Sobs again, a wracking spasm in my chest. My hands, again, the bite of nails in my palms. A scream again, a keening howl that collided with the room's distant walls and came back to me as a warbling resonance, a tragic accompaniment.

"I understand," The Boy said, his immaculate glow never fading as he spoke.

"H-he said I should come here. It was what he wanted. Before he d-died. It was what he wanted, so I came here. I—I'm sorry," I said, suddenly ashamed by my—I almost said human frailty, but that wasn't right, was it? Yet it was my frailty I was ashamed of. Whatever its source.

To distract myself from my weakness, my shame, my need, I looked around. The room was simple yet elaborate. Silk, yes, blew in an unfelt breeze, panels of golden yellow finery descending from the ceiling to just short of the floor. On them was some sort of lettering, but I couldn't see what it said, or even if it was a language I knew.

The floor was buffed and polished wood; buffed and polished, in fact, to nearly the color of the tapestries, if not their brilliance. Back against the window, the view outside still dark with the stars of lit windows and—above them—the stars in the sky itself. In front of the windows, wrapped in fabric the shade and finery of the banners, which was almost the same gold as the floor, was The Boy.

The Boy. I was looking at him, and as I did, he smiled and repeated: "I understand."

The gates yawned open again; the Valentino that had been born when Julian died felt the bellow of pain and sorrow claw up from my chest and up out of my lungs.

Then The Boy spoke again, words of wind chimes and finely tuned instruments. A voice of concerts and orchestras: "I know what happened to your Julian."

Specific, not generic, and the tears and the crying stopped. He knew. He wasn't just sympathetic, a being who knew my pain. He knew Julian, he knew me, he knew what had happened.

He might even know one of the 17 Reasons why he'd died.

"Tell me," I said.

* * *

"There are beings," The Boy began, his slender hands coming together, pearl-tipped fingertip to pearl-tipped fingertip, head bowed in preparation of what he was about to say, "all around us. Some of them surface into our awareness, emerging from their realms and domains, crossing the frequencies of our reality. These we become aware of because of their disparity, their eminence that disagrees with the fabric of what we perceive. We notice them because they are so 'different.' But there are others. . . . Yes, others," He lifted his head, eyes staring across the expanse of the room.

Even with the distance between us, I felt myself shrink down, reduce in humility, from his gaze.

"They have learned to mask their differences, to mimic the stride, the speech, the form, the habits of man, but their presence is owed to actions and interactions of a very unique and particularly disturbing dimension. You, my vampire friend, may perceive some of these beings, as you have been modified by your new existence, but others still escape your enhanced senses."

A smile on that face, a glow beyond his glow. For the first time since Julian became dust and fragments of bone in my quivering arms, I felt the darkness inside me diminish. The Boy's grin was a thing of pure and absolute beauty.

"If I could loan you my sight, you would then understand of what I speak. The air, the stuff of this reality, swims with these beings to which I refer. A face that appears to be human instead hides a shade, the extension of a great beast, a luminary from a very different spectrum. Ancient members of species tuned away from our perceptions."

The benevolence of his curled lips vanished, sliding away to a frown that spoke of sorrow in direct opposition to the grin of a few moments before. This expression spoke even before The Boy did, and the intensity made my stomach clench with terror. "Many of these are benevolent, existing, as your fellow vampires do, in harmony with others. In fact, some of them and their lives maintain the universe itself, and keep it functioning. Others, however, do not."

17 Reasons. All I cared about in that instant was one, just one.

Why did Julian have to die? Why did Julian have to die? Why did Julian have to die? Why did Julian have to die? Why did Julian have to die? Why did Julian have to die? Why did Julian have to die? Why did Julian have to die? Why did Julian have to die? Why did Julian have to die? Why did Julian have to die? Why did Julian have to die? Why did Julian have to die? Why did Julian have to die? Why did Julian have to die? Why did Julian have to die? Why did Julian have to die?

Fingernails biting into palms. "Tell me," I said.

"There are many—a great many—who occasionally pose a threat to the homogeneity of the universe. I could speak of them for years, a litany of possible horror. But you, I know, only care for one." His head bowed again, with solemnity and poise.

"They have been here, on this world, since the beginning of time. Many have sensed them, humans as well as dwellers in other realms that coexist with this one. Lights dancing in the night. Travelers deceived into wandering aimlessly between this world and the next. Human infants replaced with their changelings, parents unwittingly raising their young as their own. Tempting others into sampling their foods, and in so doing seducing them into their fold."

"Tell me," I said.

"They live among us, I can tell you that. They appear as humans, but they are not. I will speak the name of their race, and I will speak the name of the one that took your love. This is all I can do. After I reveal both of these, you must leave. I wish I could say more but there are structures that must be followed, rules that must be obeyed."

"Tell me," I said. "Tell me."

"One of these rules is that when you confront the person who took this life from you, who cut your adored one from your life, you must, without fail, utter these words: 'For The Boy.'"

"I will," I said.

"Say it. Repeat this for me."

"I'll say 'For The Boy.' Count on it. Now tell me. Tell me who killed Julian."

Then The Boy did.

* * *

Stairs down, door out. Filth greeting me as when I entered. Night welcoming me as before. A dark city revealed through headlights, streetlights, and advertising. People have spoken to me of this city, told me about "views." How you can stand in one special, secret spot and see for miles. The Golden Gate Bridge and with the slightest turn of the head the Bay Bridge as well. On a clear day you can see the Faralons, whatever they are.

They talk about the beauty of the city, the spires of the buildings, the rolling hills dotted with charming architecture: Edwardians, Victorians, and the like. They talk about the park as a swath of vermillion, a lush forest hemmed by avenues. They talk about the sun in an immaculately clear sky, making the city shine like a metropolitan jewel.

I'd never know what they were talking about. Never. My city was a dark sky, glowing windows, shining moon high above. I'd never see the bridges, just lights dancing on the towers. I'd never seen those houses except as shadowed structures.

It didn't matter. None of that mattered.

17 REASONS. A sign above a huge building in the Mission District. A puzzling sign, a cryptic sign. I had no idea what it meant. That didn't matter, either.

I said that Valentino had died when Julian turned to dust in my hands, that only a shell of myself had remained, a hollow version. That had changed.

Views didn't matter; sixteen of those reasons didn't matter.

What did matter, what was important, was what I'd learned—and what I'd become with that knowledge. Valentino was gone. What was left was pain and fury, anger and sorrow. Vengeance.

"Brother? Hey, brother. Come on, man."

I had to do research. I had to know what I was up against. Had to prepare, get ready for when I found him. Had to arm myself. Find out his weaknesses. Had to track him down. Had to know how to kill him.

"Spare change, man. Come on."

I'd do it. Certainly a steel rod up my spine. I could taste his blood in my mouth, could feel his throat in my hands. I'd break him in half, crush him until bones stuck out of his skin like needles in a pincushion. I'd push my fists into his belly and up until his heart rested in my palms, then I'd bring my fingers around it and squeeze. I'd crush his skull until his eyes left their sockets.

"Come on, you fucking faggot. Look me in the fucking eye."

Noticing him, finally: Urine and rags. Scared face, mushroomed nose, bloodshot whites, and an outstretched hand, palsied from addiction. Homeless in this century; a bum in the previous one.

I hit him in the face, fast and hard, very fast and very hard, further mushrooming his nose, blood spraying from the broken bones, the crushed cartilage. Flying back from my fist, he slammed into the bricks of the building, arms flying wide. Then down, sprawled and crying among the shit and used needles.

Then I swung around, walked away.

I had a faery to kill. A faery named Liam.

IX

Mariah had been waiting for me across the street, but when I popped the back door he just sat there, boiled eggs facing down Mission Street, oblivious to everything (including the honks and spitting Latino profanities) until I cleared my throat and said "Morgue."

Then we were on our way.

On the way, I looked out the side windows, the city sliding by. A passenger, perhaps, but a driver as well. I had taken control. I knew where to go.

If only the map were a bit more legible. Damn Pogue. Damn Pogue to hell. Watching the night scroll by, I flipped through the index cards of my mind, turned the pages of the mostly empty book, trying to remember anything, anything at all, about the species I was hunting, the individual I was pursuing.

Nothing. Or next to nothing.

Walking down a street—somewhere. Pogue in the lead, as always; me behind, as usual. He was talking, prattling on about sequoia ghosts, the redwood spirits of trees cut down before their time, how they put down roots in our world, their branches reaching out to others (or something like that) when he said something like "Fucking faeries think the world owes them for us snuffing a few of their goddamned plants."

I thought he'd been talking about me, an obtuse or cryptic burst of homophobia. I was wrong, obviously. Now I wish I hadn't just frowned and fallen a bit farther back.

Faeries. Liam. Darby O'Gill and The Little People. Men with cute accents blowing one another up. Potatoes. Freckles and red hair. Guinness. Androgyny with wings. Tinker Bell.

I didn't know anything. And since Pogue wasn't around to help, it was up to me to fill in the blanks.

The Very Bloody Marys

doi:10.1300/5329_09

For Julian.

Pain, and with it I rubbed my fingers between my eyes, rubbing the bridge of my nose, trying to massage away potential tears. Julian. My life, my love. Gone. Nothing but fragments of bone, a pile of dust at the foot of my bed.

Julian, who'd . . . was that Venice or Los Angeles? The details slid away, mixing with other places and times. He'd held my hand. I remember that. He'd held my hand, one finger sliding along my palm, a kiss without lips, a way of saying, without actually saying, *I love you*. Venice? Los Angeles? London?

Julian, who'd brought me roses, sprinkling their petals on our bed. Sheets covered by drops of red flowery velvet, a cushion for my nude body. I remember looking up at him, knowing with absolute certainty that it wouldn't get any better, that this was the man I would cherish forever. He'd been wearing . . . jeans? A tux? Nothing but a towel? The flowers, though. I remember the flowers. Clear as day.

Julian, who'd sat with me in a tiny café in Barcelona, me drinking strong Spanish coffee, he drinking a Merlot the color of fresh plasma. His lips . . . I remember his lips were lit sunsets, gleaming and crimson. He'd smiled, showing me his tiny sharpened teeth, a flirt from one nightwalker to another.

Julian, who'd shared another bottle in another city (Prague? Berlin? Athens?) with me. A tip of a narrow finger in the glass, a chime ringing pure and sweet as he circled the crystal lip, then the same finger to another lip, mine, painting me with sweet red nectar.

Julian who . . . when was that? The time he. . . . No, that wasn't it. I remember more wine, lots of wine, or was it something else? Red and tasty. Sweet and salty. The stuff of life.

Julian. When was that, when he offered me a glass of steaming, fresh, hot . . . blood? When was it? Where was it?

"Can't you go any faster?" I growled at Mariah.

* * *

"I want to see The Chef," I said to the slab of meat at the door.

"Do you have a reservation?" he answered, saying without needing to that he knew I didn't.

Not to disappoint: "No, but I'm going in anyway," I said.

"Not without a reservation, you're not," he said, stepping to put the knob behind us.

"We can do this the hard way," I said, without a clue as to what that was, but I hoped, for him, it would be something really bad, possibly involving the ripping off of limbs and the stuffing of heads into neck pipes, "or the easy way." I hoped that would be the way he'd go: opening the damned door.

The mood I was in, even if he went for the hard, I was more than willing to improvise.

"You little—" he growled, his voice sounding like rocks tumbling in a cement mixer, but he didn't get a chance to finish. The door opened behind him.

"What is it, Gazpacho?" the maître d' said, peering his slicked-back head out.

"Cold Soup was just letting me in. Official business," I said, stabbing the doorman's chest with a finger before the meat could protest. "I need to see The Chef. Now."

The doorman growled again, more rocks in a larger cement mixer. The maître d' scanned me up and down—shoes to nose and back—then said, "Come inside. I'll see if he's available."

Passing the doorman, I turned and stared hard into his ever-present shades, trying to penetrate the dark plastic and get to the eyes behind.

"I'm saving you for dessert," I said, showing him my teeth as the door closed between us.

* * *

Tables empty, barren of diners. In a shadowed corner, a lithe, weaving creature with skin the color and texture of freshly risen dough picked at a plate heaping with fried fetuses. The last time I'd been here I would have felt my last blood and vodka rise in my gullet. This time I just turned away.

Behind the maître d' I walked past more unlit candles and pristinely folded napkins. What day was it? I didn't know, and frankly didn't care. Right now I only cared about two things: a race and a name.

"Wait here," the slick little lizard said, flicking away an invisible fleck of something from his immaculate lapel, then gesturing to the same lone table I'd sat at before.

The architecture was familiar, the décor recognizable, the lighting memorable. Same tablecloths and sinks, napkin rings and gurneys, flowers in vases and institutional white walls. Eating the dead.

The same, but different. I looked around, trying to see what had changed. It was like my perspective had shifted, as if I'd lost weight, or somehow gained inches.

Same this, same that. Same room. Same table. Less clients, different time of night. It wasn't a good place; that hadn't changed. My fingers began a staccato tremble on the tablecloth, a meaningless beat, an impatient Morse. I didn't have time to sit and wait. I had to get the info I needed. Info I needed to kill a certain faery, a certain faery named Liam.

The beat stopped, the message ended. I knew what had changed, why the me of right then was so different from the me of back then. I hadn't gained anything, least of all inches in height. I'd lost something, something precious. That had changed my view of things.

Julian would have hated the place, just like I did. The velvet and gold cords, the fine silver and neatly folded napkins. The night's specials, the old favorites. Interrelationships were one thing; people one moment, then stuff for a recipe the next. But relishing it and tricking it with carefully prepared spices and techniques were quite another. A memory, darting in from an unexpected direction:

Julian and I, prowling the city, brand new officers in training for the *Conseil*. On a mission for the gruff and growling Pogue to help investigate a few tourists who'd wandered away from clicking shots of Coit Tower, the sea lions barking at Fisherman's Wharf, and the rolling hills. They'd been found in deep, dark alleys missing a few key organs.

He and I, standing under the hesitant shorts and flickers of a streetlight. On one side, a narrow canyon between two old buildings, scrawled with Chinese graffiti, smelling of fish sauce and rotting rice. The only sign of the body was a foot sticking out from between bloated trash bags. Julian had pushed the plastic aside, revealing the whiteness of the corpse. With a tear in his eye, he gestured to the precise cuts, the suddenly familiar patterning of the man's death, shank steak, rib roast, brisket, and the rest, saying: "Hunger is one thing; he was fucking ingredients."

"Good evening, sir," said a waiter, appearing at my elbow. Not my ghoul from last time, but a . . . well, not "fresh" face, as his face was anything but fresh, but a new one at least. "If you're interested I'd like to tell you about our specials this evening."

I felt my eyebrows knit. When was that? Last year? The year before? I remembered seeing the foot, the revelation of the rest of the body, the butcher's cuts. When?

One thing was certain: I was hungry. That was it; I just couldn't focus. "Just bring me a glass of the house red."

"We have an excellent vino from Napa . . ." he began, earnestness making him smile much too wide, revealing crooked rows of glistening yellow teeth.

"That'd be fine," I said. "Just bring the damned blood."

* * *

"I thought whatever business you'd had with me had been concluded," The Chef said, sitting on a stool in his kitchen-slash-laboratory. He intermittently sipped something red from a glass. Mine had been type O; his appeared to be simply wine. "Not that I don't enjoy you stopping by like this."

"The pleasure's all mine. I always like visiting this fine establishment," I said, streaking a finger along the gleaming stainless steel of a dissection table. "But I need some more information."

"Now I'm as human as the next fellow," he said, chortling at his own razor wit, being that he was the only human in the room, perhaps in the whole building (especially during daylight hours), "and so I'm more than willing to admit my faults, but I don't believe I misspoke when I said that I didn't know anything about any rogue vamps or your missing employer."

Employer was toned and delivered to reinforce my place in his world. He could call me a fucking idiot for all I cared, just as long as he gave me the information I wanted.

"You know," I said, examining the tip of my finger, pretending to be surprised by some imaginary residue on the tip, "Pogue spoke of you a lot." *He called you a fucking no-good parasite in a pretty little apron.*

"Did he now? Well, it's always nice to hear that one is thought of. What is it that Wilde said? How did it go? 'The only thing worse than being talked about is not being talked about.' Is that it?"

"Whatever," I said, shrugging.

"Now, Pogue, for all his gunpowder and barking, would have known that. Gruff, most definitely, but with a fine head on those shoulders, you could say. A man we could depend on to protect us and enforce the law. That's why I'm sure we of the night miss him and wish his safe and rapid return."

"But he's not here," I said, "and I am. So until he comes back, I'm all you've got."

"A situation that has not escaped my attention," he said with a dramatic sigh. Then, while examining the remaining few fluid inches in his glass: "But ever the optimist, I prefer to see the glass as half full. With you, Mr. Valentino, I see an opportunity to develop a new form of relationship with the authorities."

"Until Pogue comes back, that is."

"Yes, of course. Until Mr. Pogue returns to us. But until then, I want to help you in any way I can. If you have a concern with one of the other night residents of the city I hope you'll come to me for assistance."

"Oh, sure," I said. "I bet you'd have all kinds of advice."

"Assuredly. The city can be a dangerous place, even during the day. I do have some formidable contacts—as well as resources, of course."

"Resources. Well, naturally—"

"For example, I know that officers in the service of the *Conseil* receive a remuneration for their services, which can be exchanged for . . . well, let's call it 'nourishment,' since that's all it basically is, without any kind of culinary flair or panache. Nothing like what I might prepare in my humble kitchen. But what's really criminal is that not only is what you and the other officers receive fairly banal but it's also rather costly."

"Expensive."

"Exactly! Now in the course of my preparations I very often have a large percentage of . . . fluids that are simply wasted. Some, of course, I preserve for various sauces and stocks, but a great quantity is simply disposed of. It would be no great amount of work for me to simply put aside these vintages for someone such as yourself, as a gesture, you understand, for all your hard work in protecting us all from those hideous things that. . . . Well, it would do no one's appetite any good to dwell too long on them."

"Gotcha."

"So what do you say, Mr. Valentino? Would you be interested in such an arrangement sometime in the future? I really do see this as beneficial for both of us; a way for you to receive what you need to survive, and for me . . . well, I would gain nothing but the knowledge that I am helping in some small way to help those who keep the peace and make the moonlit world safe for me and my clientele."

I'd turned away from him, pretended to study a wall chart. At first I thought it was an anatomical graphic, something the coroner would use during the day. It was only after I started to really study it that I recognized the various dotted lines on the human figure, reminding me of that day (When? When? When?) in that Chinatown alley: shank steak, rib roast, brisket, and the rest. The chart was not for the coroner during the day, but rather The Chef at night.

"Tell me about faeries," I said, turning around to face him.

"I'm sorry. What did you say?" he said, blinking several times.

"Faeries. Tell me about them."

"Well, there's not much I can say about them, really. I mean, I know of them, of course; it's just that they aren't exactly a kind I see in my establishment on a regular basis. Why do you want to know? Has this something to do with the vamps you were talking about previously, or the missing Pogue perhaps?"

"Yeah," I said. "Perhaps. What do you know about them?"

"They're old. Very old. One of the ancient races, most definitely. I know they originated in Europe, Ireland specifically. The people there, the Celts, erected stone plinths and monuments to mark their territories but they are notoriously fluid in where they go and, most importantly, what they do. Mercurial, is what I'd call them. Very mercurial. As likely to harm as help, be a friend or an enemy. You know, Valentino, I could probably be of more help if you'd tell me why you need to know—"

I held up my hand. "How do you kill them?"

"Kill them? My word. What's happened? Tell me, has this anything to do with Pogue? Believe me when I say that the faery can be very dangerous and unpredictable but as far as my extensive knowledge of this world and many others is concerned I have never heard of them acting in a foolishly aggressive manner, such as attacking a member of *Le Conseil Carmin*—"

"Do you know how to kill them or not?"

"I—I don't believe I do. No, I'm positive I don't know how to harm them in any way, matter of fact. I could ask around, do some research perhaps. Maybe one or two of my more . . . outré . . . clientele might be able to offer some advice on the matter, but to be honest I doubt that they'd be willing to be made a part of such an action against them. Please, Valentino, tell me what this is about. If not for myself but for others who could be in danger if these old, strange ones have been acting inappropriately."

"I'll let you know," I said. "I have to get going. Thanks for the help." I should have kept the scorn and exasperation from my voice. I should have, but I didn't.

I was at the door, heading from one lab to the other, from his kitchen to the white-tiled dining room, when I felt his soft hand on my shoulder. Soft, but tensed and tight.

"Valentino," he said, voice rough around the edges. "Think about what we were discussing. We could have a good relationship, you and I. Mutually satisfactory, if you understand what I'm saying. An opportunity not only to have your important needs met but also for me to serve the community I care for so greatly."

I shook him off. His eyes were pale and moist in a hairless face, gleaming with calculation and no fear whatsoever. I got out my wallet, pulled out a five—leaving me only a few lonely singles—redolent with the copper bite of blood. A salary in smelly money.

Reaching down, I grabbed his right hand, brought it up, and shoved the money into it, folding clammy fingers around the bill.

"For the blood," I said. "I pay my own damned bills."

X

"Just drive," I said. I didn't need to, not at all, but I said it anyway to Mariah's greasy, wrinkled, ebony neck fat. He wouldn't have said anything, would never say anything, and I was glad he never, ever would say anything—having caught a glimpse of his eyes that one time (shudder)—but for some reason as I climbed into the backseat and he rolled away, I felt something from him, a radiance of suspicion or maybe even judgment.

He drove. I watched the cityscape scroll by, the usual flashes of streetlights and stoplights, headlights and taillights, signage and neon, silhouettes of pedestrians caught between all of that illumination and Mariah's cab. What did I care what the dead that drove thought? Look at him. On second thought, try not to look at him. He's a corpse, a stiff working a stick shift. A slab of maggoty meat clutching the wheel.

But he was there for me. Rain or shine. Well, never shine, but you get what I mean. A shiver, right then, right there: One of my best friends was a zombie cabbie.

I didn't need to say it, but I said it anyway: "Take me to the wizard." To that nothing, and again, again, again, I didn't get a response and was glad of it. I had a few other resources but since dawn was only a few hours away and I needed all the information I could get, Saul was the best option.

He was, wasn't he? I mean, sure, Pogue—that brass-buttoned asshole—hadn't left me with a lot of knowledge but what he had dribbled into my head pointed to the best places, I hoped, I prayed, to get what I wanted. The Chef had turned sour, but Saul—well, a corpse wasn't the only person I could count on as being on my side.

The Very Bloody Marys

doi:10.1300/5329_10

I hoped. Again that feeling. Was that a slight turn of his glistening, decomposing neck, a movement where no movement had been before? "I need his help," I said. "It's important."

Nothing. Nothing at all. But still a sense, an itching between my eyes. Like having the back of your head stared at, but in this case the front. It made my ass twitch, my forehead feel like it was going to blister.

"It's about Julian," I sputtered too quickly. "I know you didn't know him . . ." Then I stopped. Had Julian met my chauffeur? Had my beloved, my light, my darling, my wonder, my special, my prince, my stud, my rose, my partner, my Julian . . . had he met Mariah? Had he driven with us, on our way to and fro in the city, on official errands or just for a night out cruising the streets?

"He's dead," I said, low and slow. "Julian's dead. I need to get the people who did it. Do you understand?"

If he did, or if he didn't, he made no sign. Driving was all he did.

"He was everything to me. Everything." Saying it again made my heart blister this time. Fury pressed my nails into my palms. I wanted to rage and bellow, scream and shout, pound the back of his seat. "I'm going to get him, the one who did it. I'm going to get him."

Driving continued to be all he did.

"Saul's going to help. He has information I need."

Driving remained all he did.

"It was a faery. Do you know anything about them?"

Driving was just all he did.

"A faery named Liam. I'm going to kill him—for what he did to Julian."

Driving was what he did. Nonstop.

"I loved Julian. I loved him," I said, impending tears blurring my vision. I sniffled some of them away, got rid of the rest with my thumb, pressing so hard that fireworks went off behind my lids.

We weren't moving. We were there. Climbing out into the cool blur of the misty sunset, I started toward the house that I guessed, hoped, was Saul's newest location. Two steps, maybe three, and I turned around for some reason—catching Mariah pull away and head off into the white tumbles and misty curtains of fog. But before he vanished, obscured by the drifting pale . . . did I see? No, I couldn't have seen. But it certainly looked as if he'd turned, blistered eyes like cue balls pressed into his bloated black skin, and had been looking back at me.

* * *

Different street, different house, different door, different door knocker, my hand on the painted wood, giving the same knock. The door swung "just so" to allow a brass face of great, calm dignity.

"Hi, Abe," I said to the golem. "I need to see the wizard. It's urgent."

The statue seemed to pause. Sizing me up? I couldn't say. But just when I was going to say something, anything to get the door to open wider, it did, Lincoln stepping back with earthquake steps.

"Thanks," I said, walking in.

Down the book-lined halls, spongy old rugs underfoot. A pause of time for me to take a dozen strides, followed by a pounding behind me as Abe took up the rear.

Saul was in the kitchen again. For a moment I wondered if he'd ever left. Pogue (or had it been Julian?) told me once that for all of Saul's wrinkles and powdery white skin, frizzled hair, star-shine eyes, he was as human as the tabby cat who'd given me lip the other day. Knowledge pushed him far, far away from the rest of us, even the "us" who sipped blood and remembered when sock garters were an essential part of any man's wardrobe. Still, whatever Saul had become—however far he'd stepped sideways from even my creepy world—he was still Saul, the wizard, the magician, a source of essential information who, I hoped, could give me what I needed.

"Val, my son, what brings you back to my humble little home? More tea? I have a not-so-bad, not-so-good blend I just made up by toasting up some old Bible pages. 'Sacred but stuffy,' as my Aunt Ellen would say. That is, until that awful day she suffocated trying to breathe life into Uncle Moshe. If only they hadn't cremated him first. Tisk-tisk."

"Thanks but no thanks, Saul."

"Any word about our wayward Pogue? I must confess that I've been less than successful in tracking down those vamps you mentioned. I've had my hairy ears to the ground to listen to any murmurs about them, but the ground's been especially quiet of late."

It took me a second to realize he was talking about the Bloody Marys. They seemed a world, an age, a universe away—from back in the time before Julian had crumbled to dust right in front of me.

"That's good of you, Saul, but something more important's come up. Something I need your help on." I swallowed, hard and slow and deep. Saying the word was getting harder and harder. My emotions barbed and caught in my chest. "Faeries. What can you tell me about faeries, Saul?"

His brows knit, deeper wrinkles on the bridge of his nose. "I'm sorry; what was that, son?"

"Faeries," I repeated, heart hammering in the cage of my ribs.

"Does this have something to do with those vamps and Pogue, Val? Some new info you've gotten hold of?"

Shaking my head, I said, "No, Saul. Nothing like that. This is something else. Something more important."

Deeper wrinkles. "More important than the vanishing Pogue and rogue vamps? I'm all hairy ears, Val. Do tell. Though to be honest, I'm not too sure I'd like to know what could be worse than an officer going missing and some feral vamps roaming the streets."

"Can you help me, Saul? I need to know everything you know."

A chuckle at that. "I doubt even you have those kinds of years. But I'll do what I can. But I do have to say that I'm curious about why you need to know about our little winged friends from the Emerald Isle, though that's just something they put on the brochures since the faery kingdom is older than Ireland. Older than the Earth, some would even say, though I don't subscribe to such radical theories myself."

"Saul," I said with a slow exhalation of breath, trying to steer him back on track. "I need to know."

"About faeries?"

"Whatever you can tell me."

"Like I said, my boy, that could take quite a bit of time, but I'm sure I could pass along a digest version, a field guide, you could say, to those mercurial little sprites. How about Ten Handy Hints? Would that do you? Not graduate study but a bit better than something you'd get from sitting at your momma's knee. Not to take anything away from your beloved mother, you understand."

"Please, just tell me."

"Well, the origin of the word itself is the subject of contention, but some leading scholars have put forth some interesting theories tracing its first usage to early Mesopotamian—"

"Saul?"

"Yes, Val?"

Hooks in my throat, flames licking at my heart, tears burning the corners of my eyes. *Say it, just say it. You have to say it, if you're going to catch them and make them pay.* One word, then another: "Julian's dead, Saul. A faery did it."

"Julian?" he said, eyes wider, brighter than usual. "'Julian,' you said? That explains why you need to know, but another question remains. Who's Julian, Val? Have I met him?"

I opened my mouth, prepared to respond, but instead of words empty air just came out. My mind ran, racing around corners and into pockets of memory. Had Saul and Julian met? Had my fair-haired angel of love and beauty ever come out to this place of fog and magic? Had Julian sat in this very kitchen and sipped the wizard's strange teas? Had Julian been in Saul's moving house? Been met at the door by the mobile statuary of Abe? Had he?

I didn't know. I. Didn't. Know. It was like Julian was being murdered moment by moment, grains of memory falling through my fingers every second, minute, hour, and day. He was fading, diminishing. Being reduced down to sensations, not facts. Vagueness and not specifics. Panic, body-tightening fear. Soon he would be nothing but ghostly dreams. I had to do something. I had to do something fast.

"He was . . ." I said, trying to put into words, speech, what he was, all he meant to me. *Lover* didn't work, as it implied just heart, only body, and not soul and essence. *Boyfriend* was too frivolous and almost legal-sounding. *Soul mate* was too granola. *Everything* was best of all, but as he was evaporating from my mind, drifting away, the thought that everything that had mattered to me was gone was too much to bear. "Important to me," was all I said, blinking back tears. "Please, Saul. I need your help."

Saul was looking at me, one hand up to his right eye, fingers curled into a tube. Through the shadows there, I could see one eye, unblinking and unnaturally bright, staring at me. After an uncomfortable stretch of what could have been a full minute, he finally said, "Ah," then lowered his hand. "Faeries, eh? How do they fit into all of this, if you don't mind an old mind's curiosity?"

"They were responsible; one of them was responsible. One named Liam."

"And how do you know this, Val?"

"I—I just know. I saw it."

"You saw it?"

"I was there. He . . . aged, Saul. Fell to dust in my arms."

He took in a slow breath, closing those bright eyes for the duration. Then he opened them. "That is the way they feed, you know. Faeries. Those old tales of them tricking people into going with them, and then the people turn up ancient? Feeding time. They eat youth, consume a person's lifetime. They eat too much, and they use them all up. Just ashes left over. Tell me about Julian, Val."

I shook my head. "I can't. It's too . . . fresh in my mind, Saul. What else can you tell me about them?"

"Val . . ." he started, but then stopped, restarted: "They are old, one of the first races. There aren't many of them, but the ones that are around have been here for a long time. Like me." His laugh was rattling, coarse. Too big for such a weak joke. "They love games, and tricking people. But they really aren't all that bad. Not like some of the other things that go bump. Like this one thing, maybe you've heard of it? A species of Maladicta, lives between raindrops and feeds on profanity . . ."

"Faeries, Saul."

"Right. Well, lots of people think they can disappear, but that's not really what's going on. See, they have two forms. Two major forms, I should say, because certain other species have three or four or even sometimes a dozen. But,"—he'd seen my impatience—"most only have two. One of their usual faces, their walking-the-streets face, you could say. Pretty, very pretty. Make your heart go pitter-pat kind of beautiful. Seductive. That's the word. You know, seductive, Val? Something that makes you think that they're the most wonderful person you've ever seen? That kind of thing."

"How do I kill them, Saul?"

"Val, I—I don't know. They . . . they have two forms. Did I say that? Oy, my mind. Can't remember what century it is sometimes. Did I talk about their forms, Val?"

"You said that they have a human one, very pretty. Seductive, you said."

"Right, seductive. Very, very seductive." He paused, studying my face. "That's when they feed, taking a day or two here, a year or two there. Like I said, they usually don't drink it all up at once. Too suspicious and all that."

"They do it, Saul. I've seen it."

"Yes, so you said. Their second form is, well . . . Tinker Bell." He chuckled, lighter this time. "Tiny winged thing, usually about so big"—thumb and finger about an inch apart—"but they can get even smaller. That's why a lot of people think they vanish, but they just go real small real fast. Cute trick."

"Weaknesses," I said, beginning to see what I was dealing with. Naming it was one thing; this was more. A lot more. Liam, a tiny darting figure too miniscule to see. Liam, a haunting beauty putting his lips to Julian's lips, taking in my . . . taking in Julian's years, his months, his days, his minutes. Years, months, days, minutes he could have spent with me. With me. Not anymore.

Fury tightened my muscles, all of them. It was difficult to speak. I repeated myself: "Weaknesses." I amplified: "How can I hurt them, Saul? Tell me everything."

"Can't say, Val. I'm sorry. They're mysterious, very secretive. On other things I'm a regular font of wisdom, but faeries . . . they're slippery little things."

"Anything, Saul. Anything at all."

"Well, I've heard—heard, mind you, nothing I could say is a fact or anything. Just old wives' tales, whispers-over-the-fence-kind of stuff, nothing I'd like you to quote me on . . ."

"Saul . . ."

"They like mirrors. That's what I heard. Kind of goes with being pretty, I guess. Nothing prettier to look at than yourself. Ah, the trap of vanity, eh, Val?"

That was it. I could tell. Not a lot, barely anything, but more than I'd had when I came in. "Thanks, Saul."

"Val . . ." he began again, as if to say something else. Those bright eyes dimmed, lowered, looking down toward the blanket on his lap. Fingers, looking like they'd been carved from old birch, picked at one corner, pulling threads apart. "Be careful. That's all. Just be careful."

"I will, Saul. Thanks for everything."

Standing up, I almost bent forward to kiss his wrinkled brow but then hesitated, didn't carry through. I'd lost something important to me already. Lips to peanut forehead would be bringing him too close to me. I wasn't ready for that yet, even for just a good friend.

Toward the door, Abe earthquaking behind me, long brass legs thudding down with each step. At the door, turning the knob, opening the door, and walking out into an unfamiliar part of the indiscernible Sunset District, I didn't turn around, didn't look back.

* * *

Mariah was there in less than a minute. I slid into the backseat, and he pulled away even before I had a chance to close the door. I didn't tell him where I wanted to go, letting him drive where either I needed to go or he wanted to take me.

I didn't know a lot, but I knew more than before. Vanishing that wasn't vanishing, just shrinking down to a tiny, winged form. Feasting on time, eating years.

There had to be a way to kill one of them, to kill Liam. I'd find it, then I'd do it. That's all that mattered. Nothing else did.

Time was running out. Memories slipping between my fingers, Julian fading with each moment Liam was free.

Then: Time was running out, time different from my higher purpose. It was going to be dawn soon. I opened my mouth, about to growl to Mariah to get me home. I didn't want to hide again, to seal myself off in my windowless hole. I wanted to find Liam, feel his bones break in my fists.

About to say, but didn't. Familiar landmarks were sliding by. We were on the way there already.

Rest, then. And with the next sunset, I'd kill Liam.

XI

Coming into my neighborhood, cruising down Market, left turn onto Castro, down Castro to 18th, rest withdrew as a primary need. Gone. I hadn't been back since before Chinese, before coming up my stairs, opening my door . . . and seeing, sitting on the edge of my bed, an old man, further wrinkling, decaying, shrinking, diminishing, powdering, until there was nothing but a pair of pleading eyes in a paper-thin skull, then nothing at all but bones and dust. Julian, dead.

The moon was gone, hidden behind drifting gray clouds, but I could tell that dawn was still an hour, maybe even two, away. Out of the cab, door slamming shut behind me. I didn't want to be there. I didn't know where I wanted to be, but it was anywhere but there.

As Mariah pulled away, taillights mixing with the rest of the traffic, I jingled my keys in indecision. An hour, yes, or two, perhaps, before the sun would rise and all good vamps would, themselves, turn to dust and a few scattered bones. It was tempting, I have to say, to witness it rise, to soak up those bright, bright, bright rays. Go the way of Julian, join him wherever he was.

But I'd made a promise to his ashes and in his memory. No tan for me; but that didn't mean I had to walk up those stairs and face having to vacuum up my lover's remains. So, not home. A walk instead.

Down toward the Mission? Tempting, but it would have brought me down toward 17 Reasons and that was yet another reminder of Julian's death. So, a walk. So, a walk up rather than down.

What day was it? The Castro was all hustle and bustle. Guys out with guys, gals out with gals, plus a few comfortable straights. Tank tops, muscle tees, jeans, shorts, blond hair, dark hair, beards, mustaches, bright eyes, easy smiles. Cars cruising up and down and back and forth, the harsh little engines of scooters. The Castro, bright and

The Very Bloody Marys

doi:10.1300/5329_11

alive. Full of laughter, joy, and happiness. Up might not have been a good idea.

But then I was past it, away from the traffic and all that awful, hideous, painful joy, and into a dark neighborhood. But on those inky streets there were windows. And people. Silhouettes that touched, held, laughed, and merged together to form a single blissful whole.

Up was not a bad idea. But not just because of shadows in TV-lit apartments. In the middle of the dark neighborhood, I turned, heading I didn't know where, ending up standing under the harsh scrutiny of a streetlight. No place to go. The streets there weren't as busy. I was alone under my stern light. A few cars, back and forth. The buzzing of a few toy motorcycles. Then, I wasn't alone, because there was a voice behind me: "Heeellllooo, gorgeous!"

Cute little thing, with blond, perfect locks hanging just so over too-blue eyes, bright blue, too-tight satin shirt over a pair of spotless tan shorts, all of it straddling a cream-colored Vespa. Did I mention his smile? If I didn't, I should. If I did, I should mention it again: lots of perfect little teeth in a shapely and full-lipped mouth.

I blinked. Blinked again. Then my cheeks rosed, my face burned, my forehead flushed with embarrassment and shame. What was I doing?

"Hello," I said, clumsy, tripping over the single word like it had been an entire dictionary trying to get up my throat and out my mouth.

"Tasty treat!" he said with an easy flip of those golden locks. "Yum, yum, yum."

Somehow I was able to look away, gather myself enough to sputter: "Thanks, but I'm a bit bitter right now."

"Oh, don't say that," he said. And again that smile, brighter than the electric light over our heads. "I'm sure there's something still sweet about you."

Anger, quick and hot like being hit between the shoulder blades with a blowtorch. Not that after all my years on Earth I'd ever felt such a thing, you understand. Just an analogy for my sudden fury toward this fluffy little piece of tasty tightness. The source, not from a blowtorch, I knew instantly. Decades upon decades of loneliness, no one being there . . . except for Julian, of course. Who could forget my one true love, the man who held my hand, kissed my lips, whispered himself into my dreams, and turned sparkling eyes in my direction whenever I spoke the scintillating syllables of his name? Where were you before, my blond little package? Before Julian, before being alone?

My head hurt. No blowtorch this time, but rather a railroad spike between the eyes. Not that I had any experience with that, either, but the analogy fit too well. Bang, pound, hurt, hurt. I closed my eyes for a moment against the strike and tried to keep my balance.

Restored, I opened them again to see the clear white brightness of his smile. The time for banter was over, so I just said, "No thanks," and turned to walk away—and saw another one, this one chocolate flavored, with hair like kinked espresso, also astride a piece of Italian engineering that looked like something you'd find in a box of cereal. He also grinned at me, and licked his firm yet plush lips.

I nodded and turned away, intending to split the difference between Vanilla and Chocolate, to step off into the quiet, dark street and make my way back to my place, when two became three with a squeal of narrow tires. Out of nowhere, headlight painful brilliance as it swept toward me, the third was illuminated by the headlamps of the other two. Not chocolate, not vanilla, but maybe, could have been, possibly green tea. His ride was a knockoff, something from the land of the rising sun, just as he was. This one spoke rather than wetting his lips: "What a delicious-looking morsel," he said, never taking his eyes off of me.

"Sorry, no time to play," was what I said, as I tried to split from three, not just one or two, but as I turned my body sideways to slip between Green Tea and Chocolate, one of Chocolate's feet came off his scooter and blocked my way. As I swung my sight up from his designer tennis shoes to his too-tight jeans and then to his face to give him my best glare, Vanilla spoke, sibilants like steam leaking from a low-pressure pipe: "But there's always time to play."

I spun toward him. There on his face was mischief, play, delight, and possibly fun. Oh, where were you before? But I had a lover to avenge, plans to make, a faery to kill. I didn't have any time for mischief, play, or delight.

"Fun's fun," I said, "but I have work to do."

"All work and no play," said the blond, "makes people dull. I don't like dull."

Enough, enough, enough. "I don't care what you like or—" I began but didn't finish as Vanilla (in front of me), Chocolate (beside me), and Green Tea (also beside me) revved their tiny but more than bone-and-muscle (even vampire bone and muscle) machines. Through the rumbling of their four-stroke scooters, my thought was even louder, and comprised one word: *Crap.* Their intentions were pretty damned clear, even if their reasoning wasn't. A nasty game late at night. Three against one. Me? No experience, no weapons, no allies, no hope. Times like this I remember what Julian had told me: "When the going gets fucked, the fucked get going." Or was that Pogue? Damn this headache. Damn these kids. Damn everything and everyone.

I should have probably said something neat and witty, something cool. But I couldn't think of anything except for what I did: jump. And jump I did, spinning and leaping between Asia and Africa, between Vespa and Honda, and started to run.

Everyone's had those dreams. Right up there with falling and the bogeyman in the closet—who, according to Julian (or was it Pogue?), is actually a nice-enough being that's set itself up as a way of introducing kids to the often harsh realities of an adult world, or something like that. You're running from a creepy something, a monster from the bad part of your mind, but instead of tearing through the air, blasting with quick footsteps, you're sprinting through clear molasses, thickened air, and for every step you take, it feels like you're having to push your way through it.

A dream made real. From my first jump to the sidewalk and then away, I was shoving myself through syrup-thick air, pushing myself through atmospheric jam. As I did, all I was thinking of was a litany, a prayer of desperation. I wish I could say it was lyrical and poignant. Nope. It was just the absolute simplest: fuck, fuck, fuck, fuck . . .

Mentally fucking myself, I ran as fast as I could. I was halfway down the dark city block, the mental patter of profanity actually breaking down—from one *fuck* to the other—as I let in the idea that I might get away, but then three deep mechanical rumbles from behind, three scooters revving to life.

The hunt was on.

The corner was getting close, my fear burning away at least a bit of the syrup surrounding me. A car, then two, streaked past, and I had a fleeting idea of flagging one of them down, trying to get them to help, but just as fast as it came, it went away, chased by the idea of dragging someone else into this, possibly getting someone else killed. I was panicked, sure, but not enough (yet) to drag an innocent into it.

So, just me and my legs trying to put as much distance between them and myself. Traffic might not be a rescue but could also be a damned good obstacle, so into it I flew, hoping as I ran across the street that the traffic was fast and furious enough to keep them from staying on my tail. A screech of brakes, a yelled profanity (the same one I'd been thinking, ironically) but no bang-crash of metal and glass. I stole a look back, hoping to see one of the three laying sprawled on the street, blood pooling around him, but fortune didn't favor me and all I saw was a car spun sideways in the middle of the street, a driver stumbling out, and street scooter headlights swerving around him and his car, heading right for me.

They got closer and closer until I swear I could smell their engines' exhaust. Quickly, I ducked to one side, hoping to to make one peel off into the trees that lined the street. As I twisted and moved, one of them—flavor unknown—flashed by on my right. I saw him tear off down the street, taillights diminishing for a hundred or so feet. Then they were replaced by the blinding glare of his headlight as he turned around and headed back. Great, now I had one in front and two behind.

Not for long. As I flattened myself against a tree, another—flavor still unknown—flashed by on the sidewalk side, on my left. As he did, a sharp pain raced up my side, accompanied by a discordant, yet sharp-toned, musical score. At first I didn't know what it was, but then I saw the Bloody Mary that passed me far ahead. Outlined in the light of his buddy's headlight, I saw a chain dangling from one hand.

Two in front now, and one behind. I feigned to my right, hoping the remaining flavor would think I was going to head that way, then dodged to my left. Bad move. Very bad move. The moment I cleared the tree I was blinded by pure electrical white, the strident screaming of a small engine. I ducked to one side just in time to avoid being run down. Luckily this Mary didn't have a chain—or maybe he just hadn't pulled it out yet.

I moved back then, since all three were in front of me. Sprinting to the corner (my pissed-off driver looking up and down the road for the guy who'd run out in front of him) and to the left, I had a quick and, I hoped, good plan. I didn't want to get anyone killed, least of all, precious ol' me. I hoped the twinks wouldn't expose themselves by running me down in front of a busy city street.

I hoped, at least, but as I tore toward the distant, much busier avenue, there was a roaring in my ears. Close, damned close, and as the volume escalated, I threw myself to one side just in time. Reflexes? Damned dumb luck? Got me; but I did it just as a chain arced through the darkness, parting the air right where my head had been. Passing me, Green Tea came to an expert stop a dozen or so feet away, his chiming links spinning in a gleaming disc in one hand. The communication was clear: Don't go that way.

Screw that. I looked at him, trying my best to communicate receipt of the message, but then ran across the street, hopefully out of range of his chain, and tried again to make the safety of the neon and fluorescents of the shopping area. Problem was, during all this I'd misplaced Vanilla and Chocolate, but they knew exactly where I was. The moment I began to run across the street, a new 250-cc roar came from my right and it was all I could do to dodge it and keep from being run over by the two missing flavors.

Okay, one way was out—really out. There was no way I could pass all three of them. Not for the first time I wished that Pogue had been a better teacher, and that Julian hadn't died.

Thinking of my lost love burned a fire in my belly. Fuck this. There was no way I was going to be taken down by three swishes on scooters. No way in hell. For a second I thought about just standing my ground, taking as many of them down as I could before I was taken down myself, but then reason replaced fury. I'd have to think my way out of this.

Quickly and backwards, I ran the way I'd come. Ideas and plots zapped through my cranium. Make a weapon? Forget it. Nothing around and no time. Help? A good idea. I tried to think of a way to get Mariah to come, but drew a blank. He was just there when I needed a ride. Either rescuing me wasn't part of his job description or The Corpse That Drove was smarter than I was, and just wouldn't put himself in such a dangerous situation. Anyone else? Anyone else? I had some contacts, but the ones I could depend on were either too far away or too hard to reach.

Motors again, getting closer. I dodged between two parked cars, hoping to lose at least one of them, but the engines stayed behind me. Two more cars and I tried again, but this time one of them flashed by me, the chain rattling just above my head. It missed me by inches. *Think!* I turned to keep track of those remaining behind. A headlight was only a foot, maybe two, away from my tail and I leapt to avoid being run down only to slam into a car door. Shoulder aching *(think!)*, head swimming *(think!)*, I almost dropped to my knees from dizziness, but managed to struggle back to my feet just in time to see a rapidly approaching chocolate-shaded face. Realizing that he thought I wasn't going to get up, and that in my stumblings and shufflings I was now between two parked cars, I waited until I could see the pointed incisors before I stood up and swung my arm at what I hoped was his face or at least his throat.

Sounds like a great plan, doesn't it? But you try putting your arm into traffic. Hurts—a lot. But even though it felt like my hand was going to be ripped off, I did have the satisfaction that Chocolate was knocked around off balance to slide, skid, and tumble off his precious candy-colored machine. One down.

One down indeed. The only problem with coming up with just one plan is that it's inadequate when you have more than one problem. All of my problems made themselves known when I heard a roar to the right and then to the left, with me in the middle. I guess it didn't matter which way I turned, because that would have left me exposed to the other direction, but, for the record, I twisted right—so I got slammed in the back of the head from the left.

No stars, no tweeting birds, just a lot (and I do mean a lot) of pain, knocking me right down to my knees. I also threw up. Just as I brought my head up, there was one of them, Vanilla, still sitting on the seat of his bike, grinning wide and happy. Then he smiled wider, teeth revealing themselves in greater detail. He might have been vanilla on the outside, topped with bright gold and perfect little features, but down deep, where his heart should have been beating, he was nothing like that.

I knew what he was, because I was one as well.

Introductions weren't necessary. I knew him, recognizing him and his buddies even through my swirling and pounding concussion due to our common dentistry. They knew who I was, as well. Valentino, Meet Mary; Mary, Meet Valentino. And the others? Plural. Sweet young things full of flirt and tease, grins hiding sharp teeth. Valentino, Meet the Bloody Marys, the (ahem) Very Bloody Marys.

Proudly displaying his ill-gotten incisors, Vanilla lisped: "Another sickly, pale little vamp," he said, tisk-tisking his golden locks side to side. "I know just what you need."

Just as I was going to do something stupid, like ask him what he meant, my lights went out completely.

XII

Consciousness sucks. At least, coming back to it and remembering how you lost it in the first place does. How humiliating. How uncomfortable: gravel digging into my back, my head at a weird angle.

Where was I? Rubbing my knocked noggin, I pulled myself up, stood, looked around. It was still night, though not the deep, dark, blackness that had been there when I'd been knocked on my ass. Stars above, but their twinkling was beginning to dim. It was the time of night for all good vamps to be back in their crypts, tombs, or windowless apartments.

But that's definitely where I wasn't. The gravel was on the roof of a building. The weird angle my head had been at was due to an air conditioner vent. I was at least ten floors up. Stretching, getting my kinks out, I turned slowly, surveying. The building was alone, not connected to any others. In front of me was a taller one, separated from mine by a wide alley, the wall facing me nothing but a monolith of bricks unbroken by windows. Every other side was a busy street. Aside from my air conditioner vent there was a roof access door of battered, but still very strong, steel. Nothing but a fixed handle and a keyhole. It would swing out, the hinges being on the inside. Nothing else.

Ten floors up was impossible. I could jump, certainly, but I'd be nothing but a smear when I landed. One of the benefits of being a "night person" was great healing capacity, but there's no healing from a splat. I was tempted for a few hummingbird beats of my frightened heart. Risk it all on gravity, but then I chickened out—or smartened up, depending on how you looked at it.

I probably could have figured out a way down if I'd had the time. Maybe crawl down the side of the building until I got to a window, or worked on the door.

The Very Bloody Marys

doi:10.1300/5329_12

Probably. Maybe. But I didn't have the time. Oh, crap. That's what the Bloody Mary meant by working on my tan. There was nothing on the roof but gravel, the door, and a vent—and the sun was coming up.

* * *

Apples. Piles of them in broken-slatted barrels or unraveling baskets. Little red things, usually with at least one bruise. Never perfect, not like the ones you see these days in supermarkets. A few that had tumbled down between the cobblestones descended in freedom only to be mashed to pale smears, appealing only to flies.

The Market. That's all we ever called it. It had another name but that's long gone from memory. Salvatori, who sold those apples in front of my building, said you could see the Vatican from our street. I tried a few times, convincing myself that if we could see it, they could see our street. An inadvertent blessing by some priest or maybe even the Holy Father himself, looking out a leaded glass window, out at the city—blessing our street with an admiration for the view.

But then I saw something else, and gave up trying to see the dome and the spires of the Holy City, instead focusing on not stepping on crushed fruit. Red apples and golden piss. Sitting on the curb, watching the world pass me by, a look to one side at the old man and his baskets and barrels, urine staining his pants, dripping, pooling on the ground. Too lost to notice, too mad to care.

After that I stole apples from Salvatori whenever I could. He'd scream if he saw me do it, but after a while he stopped even doing that, maybe guessing that it was a fair trade for stealing my innocence and hope that my street was anything special. It was just one of thousands in Roma, but I knew that day that the place where I lived was worst than most.

Funny what you think of as the sky brightens for the first time in . . . when was it? Never good at dates. Not much good for anything, according to Momma. Boneto, whose head gleamed like fresh marble, sharpening knives on a spinning stone wheel set on the side of his pushcart. Sparks bright even in high daylight. Forrenti, quivering hands pawing through glistening sausages, listlessly fluttering them at the persistent flies that were his best customers. Valtali, the cobbler, crouched on a scratchy blanket, his own fingers deft and quick, the closest thing to magic I'd seen. Nails appearing between his crooked fingers then vanishing into the soles of the shoes he'd been asked to fix, the ringing of his work clearer and louder than the nearest church bell. I'd sit and watch him for hours, waiting for him to miss, though he never did. Passerelli, who sold day-, week-, or even month-old bread, laughing like summer thunder, slapping his belly at the telling or joy at hearing each and every joke. Walking up and down, one end of the market to the other, I'd be their son: Boneto, whose eyes could see the smallest nick or imperfection in the finest steel; Forrenti, whose sickly sweet smell and bad teeth were on the outside of a saintly soul; Valtali, whose hands were quicker than anyone's eye; Passerelli, who roared with joy at the world around him.

Or I was the sire of a distant land. But books were for those with money, or who could read, so I didn't use that one a lot, my imagination being more comfortable with being the son of drunks, madmen, or failures. I passed one summer thinking I was the son of God, but our local priest, Father Delprissi, who always made it a point of not walking down our street, caught me trying to cure Forrenti's palsy, and slapped me hard enough to loosen a tooth.

* * *

Pushing flat against the vent, hyperventilating and biting my lip, I watched the sun peek over the ragged teeth of the skyline in the East. As it chased my nightly safety blanket away, changing a black and white world to one of burning color, I saw my first view in at least one hundred years. And you know what? It was nice and all, but not worth dying over.

Shadows. Don't really see many of those when you become a night person. But there they were, stretching out from the features on my otherwise featureless rooftop. The door's was twisted, the triangle shade narrowing until there was nothing but a gray sliver of safety.

I'd thought about hiding there but at the last second had decided on crouching behind the vent instead. Lucky. If I hadn't, I'd be smoldering, blistering, crisping, ashes and smoke. Bye-bye. Nice knowing you.

Still might. Oh, shit; oh, Christ; oh, fuck. It was moving: My narrow margin of bright light and shadow was shrinking. Looking down at my feet, fingers splayed out on the gravel for balance next to them, I could see the edge, the line between shade and sunlight melting slowly away.

Lower, a tighter ball. My back was hot. Was it burning? Burning? Burning? No, just hot. Only hot—for now. Breaths in, breaths out. I tried to keep my terror from screaming, my fear from crying.

The sun rose higher.

* * *

Yeah, sure, Momma could have been a bit more nurturing, a tad more caring, baked me cookies, or read me a bedtime story—when she wasn't beating me with a length of coarse, stiff rope she kept hanging behind our apartment's front door. It just wasn't who she was. Drinking cheap wine until she had to stumble down to the hall to the bathroom, making it only some of the time, to loudly puke it all back up; that was closer to what she was. Still, it could have been worse. How much worse, I have no idea, but the thought of anything worse still keeps me awake with shivers and shakes.

As soon as I was old enough, I moved out. Well, to be honest, as soon as I was old enough, I ran out—since all I had was what I had on and a black eye. My street was a nice enough place to grow up. All the apples I could steal, water from the fountain at one end, a warehouse where I could sleep at the other, thanks to a very drunk Sicilian night watchman.

I saw Momma every once and a while, stumbling here, falling over there. If I saw her first I usually would duck into the nearest doorway or under the closest table—lots of fun if I was loitering near the Villa Romana, the closest the Market had to a good place to eat. There the food was cheap and foul, the wine bitter and harsh, and the seating tight and intimate—not good cover for a kid hiding from a shrieking madwoman.

If she saw me first then I usually ended up sleeping differently that night, favoring a different side or whimpering while I cradled a wrenched arm or kicked thigh. Between blows, and yelling my name, she'd say the same thing over and over. So much so I wondered if it was part of the family crest, a legacy from my father: *Niente*. Making me the son of nothing, heir to nothing, inheritor of nothing, and, if Momma hadn't been drinking all that much and was a bit more articulate, worse than nothing.

Two hundred years later and I'm starting to realize she may have been on to something.

* * *

Smoke. I smelled smoke. The moment I smelled it, I felt it. My back was burning. Whimpering in fear and with the memory of that rope tearing into my back, I pushed myself down, away from the sunlight tipping over the top of the vent. The pain ebbed but didn't completely go away. If I'd been wearing a coat, some kind of protection other than shirt and jeans. . . . But I wasn't, and so I blistered, smoked, and burned.

My vision wavered, an aquarium view of my feet and hands. The gravel was bright and clear, even through my tears. It was hard to believe I'd spent time in this too-focused world. When you live at night, the world is small and close, as big as the nearest illumination.

Smoke again, burning again, and with a pathetic whimper I pulled myself down even tighter, knees grinding into the gravel's teeth, each sharp stone, each tiny rock apparent through the stabbing pain in my knees. Instead of looking at the shrinking of my shade, paying too much attention to my baking flesh, I twisted my neck, turned my head, and looked out at the city. But then I went back to watching my death crawl across the roof. The world of the sun was too big, too clear, too expansive.

And the cost for the view was just too damned high.

* * *

I don't know my birthday. I thought about making it Christmas Day, but after Father Delprissi's slap, I decided that Jesus didn't want me anywhere near him. What I miss about not having a birthday has nothing to do with presents or noisemakers, icing on cakes, and all that. But when I think about things back in Roma, about young

Valentino, I have to use markers like "that time it was so cold that cats froze stiff," or "when Salvatori finally went completely crazy, so they took him away." Landmarks of the weather, deaths, births, disasters—not something simple like a month, a day, a year.

When the hills burned. That's when it was. The old ladies who shuffled back and forth, they looked up at the bleeding sunset and crossed themselves, mumbling Jesus' name while clicking their rosaries to hold back the end of the world.

A farmer who came to our street to sell his ulcerous and ugly tomatoes said it was a fire up in the hills, the smoke staining the sun as it set. Not the end of the world, just some fool who didn't know how to put his campfire out. Not Satan, not weeping Jesus; just an idiot who didn't use enough water, didn't stir his ashes.

Just a fool. Not a saint or a sinner. Just a fool. And still the world changed.

One of my poor hiding places had become one of a half dozen small jobs that kept more than just apples in my belly, even if what kept my stomach from complaining was leftovers from Villa Romana. One night as I moved boxes, swept the cobblestones, and did whatever else Mr. Esposito, the owner, wanted me to do, I for once didn't keep my head hung down low. I looked up.

Word of advice. It might be tempting to look up, to look out at the world beyond your tiny space. But resist. Fight it. I didn't, and saw something worse than an inflamed sky: a smile.

Short, I remember that. The light had faded, the wine-red sun having completed its setting, giving itself up to a warm summer night, the stars having come out to wink mischievously down at us, and he was standing across the street in a dull pool of weak light spilling from the whorehouse next to Villa Romana. Stocky as well as short, burly, swarthy. Hair, I remember, kinky and tightly curled. He could have been Greek; he could have been from an even deeper, darker part of Sicily than even the drunk who guarded the warehouse.

I glanced from my sweeping, my hauling, and saw him there. He smiled. I didn't know when my birthday was, but that was a nice gift that day. A grin of pleasure from him to me.

Next door there was drunken laughter, the catcalls, and the bitch fights. I didn't have enough to afford even a wink, but I wasn't interested in catching their eyes. The women all looked . . . wrong somehow, like they were trying to be something they weren't. I had an idea of how it all worked; I'd seen Momma pull a few when she thought I was asleep, or just didn't care that I wasn't, but looking at them, I didn't feel anything but puzzlement.

But then he stood across the street from where I was working, and smiled, then winked, and I felt something. I think I dropped my broom or the crate I was supposed to be carrying, but those nerves have jingled my memory, and now all I can remember is the night the hills were burning and him standing there—the first person who was happy to see me.

Work ended (even though I was sure it never would), Mr. Esposito slapping my back as he flipped a few dull lira into my dirty hands. I didn't care how many, I didn't care about what he was saying, all I wanted was to be out of there, and across the street.

After I'd seen him, and he'd seen me, he'd melted back into the shadows of the alley. Lifting, sweeping, I'd steal looks to make sure he was still there. Every time I was sure he'd gone, faded completely into the darkness between the buildings, a match would flare and a cigarette would glow, revealing the heavy face, the tight twists of his hair, or a wayward flash of illumination from the whorehouse would show tight, firm lips pulled up into a pleasant expression of mirth.

Crossing that street was the longest few strides I'd ever made, suspense and jitters stretching seconds into gooey minutes. But I was there. Seeing me see him, he pushed himself up off the barrel he'd been leaning against, greeting me with a flip of a meaty wrist.

He said something quick and light. I said something clumsy and forced back. He offered me a cigarette, a tight curl of dark brown paper packed tight with foul leaves and awful tars. I took it, lit the end from the glowing tip of his, and wracked painfully after my first draw.

Thunder, low and quaking—that was his laugh as he slapped my back. Spitting and gagging, that's what I was doing.

"Bello," was what he said after I stopped coughing. I let the cigarette fall to the ground in a tiny meteor of sparks, and turned my eyes

to his. *"Bello,"* he said again, rough hand coming up to stroke my cheek. *"Molto."*

I didn't know what to expect. I couldn't afford fantasies, and information had been dribbled here and there from loud old men and crazies like Salvatori, and shame was whispered in my ear by priests. I knew my body was doing something—urgently, persistently, dramatically—but I didn't know what to do with it.

So I followed it, and him, into the warm summer darkness between the old buildings. A background perfume of piss and vomit swirled around us as he ran a hand down my chest, his breath—stale and reminiscent of cheap wine and stifling smoke—puffing gently into my face, the sweetest thing I had ever smelled.

I didn't know what to expect. No fantasies, little information, much ignorance, lots of guilt; nothing but this man who'd seen me and liked what he saw. A real treasure for the boy who had nothing at all. I think I would have done anything for him.

Then he grabbed my hair, pulled my head back, and bit me.

XIII

My finger was on fire. One moment it wasn't, then the shade had retreated just enough, the sun encroached—again, just enough—for light to hit the edge of my left hand's little finger.

All screamed out, I hissed instead, jerking my hand away from the harsh illumination and beating out the flames against my shirt. And for a brutal moment my balance went bye-bye and I began to tumble out of the shade and into a flaming death.

My mind was dead white, a rage of fear and static, but my body didn't want to burst, split, and turn to ash. It saved me when my mind couldn't, muscles acting without permission (thank god), throwing me back with a bruising gong against the steel of the vent.

Safe for a moment, I wrapped my crisped little finger in my shirt and whimpered in pain, but then my elbow came out, was seen by the sun, and skin blistered and crisped there, too.

With more whimpering, more hissing, I pushed myself harder against the steel, as the day inched ever closer.

* * *

I should have died, of course. He should have eaten and run, leaving me dead and drained in that little Roman alley. But then someone saw us: a pair of soldiers who thought my street could have been, in some way, fun for the night. Seeing him and me together, one holding the other, lips to neck, they'd leapt to defend their tenuous heterosexuality, fists cracking into our bones.

He'd run away; to where, I have no idea. Never heard from him again. Such a guy: Do me, then not stick around for breakfast. A few pints low, I sagged, I swooned, I drooped, and couldn't go anywhere, especially not quickly, like my would-be paramour did after he broke two of my ribs, my nose, and my hand. But that's not what hurt.

The Very Bloody Marys

doi:10.1300/5329_13

Okay, that hurt, but it wasn't as painful as a few hours later when my previous old pal, the sun, rose over the rooftops and my shaded little alley became, well, a rooftop at high noon.

Even though I never went to school, I like to think I'm a fast learner. I mean, when you stagger up from being beaten into a near coma and find your hand combusting with the first touch of sunlight, it doesn't take a Marconi to figure out something odd is going on.

It took me about a week to get the hang of it. I'd heard of what I was . . . and I don't mean the kind of man who goes into alleys with other men. But like everything else, it took me a while to separate the cream from the blood. The basics I got pretty quickly. Sunlight bad; very, very bad. Nothing tasted good—except for blood—and there was a big problem with that.

I was a coward.

* * *

I hate hot. Hate it a lot. Hate it when I sweat, hate it when every breath feels like sucking the air out of an oven set to INFERNAL. Hate it especially when I am wrapped around an air conditioner vent in the fetal position while daylight inches and inches and inches closer. I missed the night. I missed cool. I missed a world defined by headlights, streetlights, neon, and incandescents. I missed darkness.

My back was getting warm. Too warm. I knew some brilliance, some brightness was peeking over the top of my steel-box sanctuary and was touching my clothed back. How long until it filtered through? How long until I wasn't just warm but was burning, flaming, crisped, and dead?

Night is too short; day is much too long.

* * *

I craved it; my stomach growled and demanded it. I got close, a couple of times, stalking some stumbling drunk, inching my way up to him—wondering how to hold him while I sank my baby teeth into his neck. But each and every time I squawked, I laid an egg right there in the street and flapped my wings back into the shadows.

Ever sucked the blood from a cow? How about a kitty cat? A nice little puppy dog? A horse? I, for one, recommend the cow, even though they are a bit hard to find in most cities. The problem with country living is there just aren't a lot of places to hide out during the day.

I thought at first about trying to stay home, but that quickly proved to be a mistake. Going into an alley with someone was bad enough, but to tell the wrinkled, smelly old men who sort of raised you that you are now a . . . well, one of "those" guys? Every time the subject inched toward confession, someone would interrupt my little heart-to-heart with something like "Did you hear about the cow on the such-and-such street, how they almost caught the guy biting it?" or "I miss my poor cat so much," and I'd just nod and say "How awful" or "That's sick," or agree when they talked about lynching the sick son of a bitch.

But there was something else. Certainly, I was more than a bit . . . well, paranoid is a little understated. It wasn't that I thought everyone was out to get me, but resorting to sipping from whatever animals I could find, dodging the daylight world, I began to feel like everyone and everything, well, didn't have my best interests in mind. Put it that way.

Sure I thought about just crawling up onto a rooftop and watching the dawn break, and toasting myself to a lovely charcoal, but that's the thing about cowardice: when you have it bad enough you can't even think about ending it. That takes bravery.

So I left town, and, as it turns out, was damned lucky I did.

* * *

They lied. Twenty-four hours in a day—twelve night, twelve day, they said. But that's not right; it couldn't be right. They must have slipped in some extra hours or minutes in there somewhere. It was the only thing that made sense.

Either that, or this day would never end, or would end when the sun finally peaked fully over the top of the vent and I burst completely into flame.

And that would be nighty-night for me. My last.

* * *

I won't bore you with the travelogue. The sights weren't all that spectacular, the meals mostly four-legged and still living, and villagers not at all welcoming, what with the torches and all that. Moving by night, having to avoid the day, is not a great way to travel. It's one thing to have twenty-four hours to play with, but with a sunlight death sentence it meant that every time dawn started to break, it was a new scuttle for a dark room, a crypt with a few loose hinges or a crappy lock, and an abandoned fill-in-the-blank.

I learned a few important lessons on my way out of Italy and to the United States in the hold of a very slow freighter with more than its fair share of juicy rats. I learned that I wasn't alone, and that the creatures who shared my scuttling and twilight new world weren't going to be of much help. I remember one dryad who'd taken up residence in an old armoire I came across in Prague, who said it very well, in a voice that sounded like a pair of rusty old hinges wheezing out each word: "We're separate, not just from the humans, but from each other as well."

But there was something else, too, more than the other odd things I'd stumbled across going from Point A (Rome) to Point B (wherever I was headed). One vamp, in particular. Called himself the Baron, though it was obviously a title by accent and acting and not by blood. A sad old man, bitten while in his sixties and therefore trapped at that age, he'd served me my first human blood, a vintage poured from a bottle, and told me that odd things were happening in my new world, something that I should be concerned about. . . . No, frightened of.

That was enough for me. Or at least it was until I came back to his place after running some errands for the old man and found him dead, head neatly removed from his body. I'll never forget his expression—and not just because it was staring at me from the table in front of his body. It takes a lot to frighten a vampire—and he'd been terrified.

New York was nice, but trying to find a bite (sorry about that) to eat was tough, so tough I was shot five times and beaten to a pulp every other day. I got the hint and got out of Dodge. Went west. Funny, but now when I catch shows on the tube about that time, they always talk about the Civil War, the Emancipation Proclamation,

Ford's Theater, but to me it was cellars, freight yards, holds of tramp steamers, warehouses, rafters, and fear. Lots and lots of fear. They might be scared of me, the men and women who might happen to spot me during my dietary necessities, but I was far more scared of them, and whatever else was out there.

In Chicago, I lost my virginity. No, not that kind; I had lost that decades before. No, this was a different kind of first: I killed someone. I was indulging in a bit of "that" kind with a hick who worked the stockyards. He was okay in bed, though we never got close to real intimacy, but blowing him for all the blood I could haul away had its advantages. But then one day one of his buddies walked into the wrong room at the wrong time.

My prince was hardly charming. In fact, his fists hit the hardest of all, broke the most bones, and drew the most blood. That is, until I looked up from the cement floor of the slaughterhouse, not knowing how much of the red sticky stuff on my face, chest, and hands was mine or the cow's, and saw him smiling down at me as he picked up a crowbar, weighing it by slapping it into his meaty hands.

When I came back from the frightening place—the red-tinged domain of my fists ramming into their chests, their legs and arms snapping, my endless roaring—his friend was dead, the crowbar having crushed his skull, propelling his eyes across the room. He was staring up at me as I tore into his throat, drinking long and deep. I could have stopped. I could have let go, dropped him to the floor, and walked away. But if I did, he'd turn out just like me. So I killed him. I like to think it was merciful, saving him from vamping, rather than just wanting to see him dead. I'd like to, but I can't be certain.

* * *

Smoke. I could smell it. Reminded me of Chicago, the barbecue aroma of burning pigs. No pain, at least not yet, but I knew that some new part of me was burning, turning to ash and maybe even crumbling bone.

I didn't move. I knew if I did I wouldn't be able to stop—a flaming meteor streaking across the roof of a building in San Francisco, a crumbling, tumbling skeleton, and a rolling wave of smoke and crisped debris. That would happen if I did move. So I didn't.

I just didn't.

* * *

I've been in the city for . . . how long? God, it doesn't seem that long. Such a big number. Strange how time can just slip by you. Half the time I don't know whether I like this place or I am just tired of running from one place to another. But there I was, a century just beginning and me starting to wonder how many more I'd end up seeing before either some cocksucker whose cock I sucked split my skull, or the bogeymen caught up to me. I remember sitting down by the docks, watching the fireworks and wondering what was going to happen, whether my personal rocket was on the way up, or had burned out without my even noticing on its way down.

By the 1950s I was haunting a local hospital, night shift of course. It was an easy job, a shit job: emptying bed pans and cleaning toilets. But it kept me where blood was. A sip here and there, a bottle or two missing, and I was a happy little vamp. I thought for the first time in decades that things were looking up. I even had a little spending money, and there was always some way to have a gay old time on Saturday nights.

One of my first major purchases was a record player. Not top of the line but fancy enough. And with it, of course, the need to buy records. I was in one of my favorites, a dusty little shop on Market Street, flipping through pressed vinyl looking for something stirring and operatic, when the hairs stood up on the back of my neck.

"We need to talk, boy," said this lantern-jawed bit of military hardware, his posture saying that I didn't have a choice.

Valentino, meet Pogue.

* * *

I didn't want to believe it. I just didn't. It was too much to hope. So much had gone wrong, so much I'd screwed up. For this to be even possibly happening was just too much to hope for.

But, still, that's what it looked like. Just to make sure, I kept my eyes fixed on the meridian line, the demarcation between blasting daylight and my precious shade. I watched it until my eyes felt like I could have been staring into the furnace that was above me. I didn't blink. I didn't dare.

It was too good to be true, but that's what seemed to be happening. The sun was going down.

* * *

"Let me tell you how it is. Short and sweet."

And he did, explaining the law of the land, and where I fit into it all. I was alive, or allowed to exist at least, because I'd walked softly—sipping rather than drinking from necks, a kind and contentious vamp, not a rapid killer. I'd escaped what I'd felt nipping at my heels, the dread following every vamp on the planet, the *Conseil*'s purging of most of the other bloodsuckers, by cowardice and dumb luck. They didn't want a trainee who'd be tempted by all those juicy necks. Naturally, I felt relieved. Naturally, I also felt even more humiliated.

Pogue and a few more years, learning what he wanted to teach me about my new world, working for Blood Money with which to buy a glass or two of the red stuff, my little windowless apartment, Saul and The Chef, the other sideways, twisted, underground, and shadowy residents of the city.

Leading from there to here, the past rolling behind me, the future sitting in front of me. One more night, and as my precious shade lengthened, stretched, and faded into the background of twilight, I knew this was going to be the best night of my little, pathetic, very extended life, just because I was alive to see it.

* * *

But sewn through it all, woven between recollections and memories, jammed between good times and bad, blood, fear, panic, and brushes with too many dawns, there he was, a ghost haunting my past, a specter of love and life. Slippery when I tried to hold onto him, an aching pain when I thought about his dust and crumbling bones in my arms: Julian.

After an hour, perhaps two, it was dark enough for me to stand up. My body was sore, my back badly burned and sore from keeping the same position for twelve hours, my finger throbbing in agony, but I was alive and it felt good.

Getting down would be a challenge, but I wasn't worried; I had time to plot and plan, think rather than react.

A faery named Liam. A missing boss. Three twinks on Vespas. I had a lot to do. But before I began to search for a way down, before I started to put it all in order, get on with things, I turned and looked out at the evening sky, where the sun had set behind the buildings, making its way below the horizon. So many years. So many years as Valentino the vampire, Valentino the coward, Valentino the pathetic fag, Valentino the screwup, Valentino the failure.

Bye-bye, sun. Let's not do this again soon. Still, in a weird way, I was glad it'd happened. I might be Valentino the vampire, but bye-bye, Valentino the coward, bye-bye, Valentino the pathetic fag, bye-bye, Valentino the screwup, bye-bye, Valentino the failure.

I had things to do, but not for Pogue, not for the *Conseil,* and—as I thought it, I felt a stab of pain and loss—not even for my beloved Julian.

For me.

Bye-bye, sun. Hello, night.

XIV

Getting down was a trick, but one I was able to abracadabra with a certain degree of presto and change-o, and oh-so-stylish hocus-pocus. Okay, it wasn't exactly magic, but it worked: I banged on the door until someone came up to see what all the fuss was about.

"Locked out," I told the bathroom-slippered matron, flashing her my if-not-winning-then-second-runner-up smile and patting her on the top of her blue-rinsed head. She must have bought my innocent act because she didn't use the Louisville Slugger she clutched in her pale-boned hands.

Down the stairs and out. Where the hell was I? Ah, there it came, the map of the city all we residents carry in our heads. A sad bit of architecture on the hill above the Tenderloin but below Nob Hill—or as I've heard it described, fondly and not, the Tenderknob. Surrounded by more regal edifices, my would-be final resting place was skinned with peeling paint and graffiti to the point where the gangs wouldn't have been able to make out their own signatures. The entryway was dark, most of the foyer bulbs burnt out or broken.

Not a great place to live, and definitely not a great place to die. So glad I didn't have to do either.

Where now? The list was long, but the night was young. Taking a long, slow breath to calm the nerves that still rang and jangled in my ears from my brush with dawn, I tried to inventory the contents of my skull. Ever seen a snow globe? That's what was between my ears.

Like one of those novelty trinkets, though, my mind was still basically clear. Okay, there was swirly stuff going around inside, but I could see through it all, out to where I needed to go.

Never a cab around when you need one. Guess Mariah was getting his tires rotated, his eyes squeegeed, his blood changed, his hide pol-

The Very Bloody Marys

doi:10.1300/5329_14

ished, or whatever it is zombie cabbies do when they aren't doing their damned job. So I started walking.

I'll tell ya, after a few long strides, I was glad he wasn't there. After you spend twelve hours curled into a fetal ball while the blast furnace of a bright summer's day crawls by and over you, stretching your legs is too damned magnificent.

Ah, better than a lot of things; too good to even bother giving up the brain power enjoying it to think about what it was as great as. The night was cool too, which took away even more brain power. On the corner, I stopped, just letting the chill race over my still-damp shirt and jeans, biting my goose bumps with playful nips. Traffic was light, just streetlights and the cold blue glows of TVs in apartments to light my way. The quiet street shook up my snow globe, the flakes of fear getting agitated once again. All it would have taken would have been the 250-cc hornet buzz of a Vespa to make me jump straight out of my skin.

Nothing but cold dark, nothing up and down and back up the street. No scooters, no Green Tea, no Vanilla, no Chocolate, no Marys—Bloody or otherwise. Deep breath again, legs moving again.

Bit of a walk to where I was going, but, like I said, walking felt great, walking felt tremendous, walking felt incredible. But as I did more of it, the novelty thinned just enough for a new thought to work its way in among the exalting *great, tremendous,* and *incredible,* the one thing walking was better than. I would have said "being alive," but that's not quite right. Call it not burnt up, not ashes and soot—not being dead.

So, not being dead, not being cramped and curled, I came down from that hill, hit and then crossed the quickly flowing chrome and roaring motors of Market Street and headed to the left, toward the Mission.

The Mission and 17 Reasons, 17 Reasons and The Boy. I knew I had other responsibilities, way too much to do (including catching the ferocious little twinks that tried to give me a deep-down tan), but for some reason the most important thing in my mind was getting back to The Boy to tell him what had changed . . . and what hadn't changed at all.

A few more blocks and more than just being alive, walking, and the cold night felt good. It was like I'd just awakened from a bad sleep. Coffee has nothing over almost dying.

As I got closer I began to rehearse what I'd tell him when I got to 17 Reasons, a speech of explanation, a way to try to put out to him in the form of words how the Valentino that'd been there last was gone, that a new one was there in front of him—one that would do what he asked, but not for The Boy, not even for my precious Julian. I'd do it because it was my job. I was a cop. I'd do it for me. No longer revenge: justice.

A few blocks from there, stopping on another corner but this time to pant (a bit) and wheeze (a bit more), thoughts still running through my snow globe about what I'd say, how I'd say it, and what might happen when I did, I realized with a longer (by more than a bit) sigh that I might not have that chance.

A face from the darker shades of a recessed doorway next to me; from the face a sly smile; out of a sly smile, a scintillating voice, a melodic sing-song in a whispering contralto:

"Monsieur Valentino. As always, a pleasure to see you again, *n'est-ce pas?*"

Oh, shit.

* * *

The inky blackness didn't so much as run as steadily walk out of that doorway. A pooling, a billowing, a smoking, and then up and into arms and legs and a wide-brimmed hat pulled down over hooded eyes.

"Hello, Ombre. What brings you back?" I said, wanting more than anything on God's black night not to be there right then.

"I did not leave, Monsieur Valentino. The *Conseil* trusted me—just as it trusted you—to perform my duties, and that is what I shall do."

Ever try to read ink when it isn't making nice neat letters? The *Conseil* agent was pulling his best Rorschach test, a blot that told me more about my own impatience than what his presence was all about.

"Ombre . . ." I began, but shifted gears from suddenly roaring mad to what I hoped he'd read as neutral. "Things have been a bit . . . odd. But I'm on it. Really."

"May I ask, Monsieur, for a bit of indulgence then? You see, it would be beneficial, for both of us, to present to our superiors a report of what we have uncovered regarding the rogue vamps and . . . I take it that you have had no fortune on locating Pogue, eh?"

"No. No luck so far, I'm sorry to say."

"As I am sorry to hear. Then perhaps you've made progress in locating and, may I hope to say, eliminating, the so-called Bloody Marys?"

Did my hand go up to my face? Did I shiver and shake, pulling my elbows in close and touching my chin to my chest? Did my eyes widen, forehead wrinkling? Did I wrap my arms around myself, a long-limbed safety blanket? Did I do any of that possibly betraying stuff as I flashed back to my pleasant day spent on a rooftop, when I realized that seeing a few rays after a hundred or so years just wasn't worth dying for?

"We've . . . met," I managed to say, coughing roof dust into my fist. "I'll take care of them. Don't worry." I meant that, even if it wasn't high on my list of priorities at exactly that moment.

Maurice Chevalier, Louis Jordan, Claude Rains, Jean Reno might have seen my body do its little shudder and shake dance of memory, or maybe Monsieur Ombre had seen something else. But one thing (okay, maybe two or even three things) was clear: he'd seen something more in me because those narrow eyes narrowed a bit more as he stared at me from under the velvet of his shadowy hat.

"Valentino," he said, and instantly I missed his slimy and condescending *Monsieur*. "I perhaps may be mistaken but I detect a . . . change in you, *non*? Has anything occurred to you that perhaps I and, through me, the *Conseil,* should be aware of?"

"No," I lied, "nothing's happened. Nothing worth reporting to the *Conseil,* at any rate."

Maurice, Louis, Claude, and Jean's eyes narrowed even further, until all that showed of them was a sliver of gleam. It felt like I was being X-rayed and, what with Ombre and his shaded, shadowy, inky, black-wrapped self, I might as well have been.

Don't ask me where the lie came from. I should have told him, I know—but told him what? That Julian was dead, drained of life and his precious young years by a faery from the land of shamrocks and green beer? That I'd let a gang of flavor-of-the-month faeries from the land of J.Crew and Tommy Hilfiger catch me and leave me to die on some tenement roof? That I'd been on the way to a building in the Mission District with the cryptic sign of 17 Reasons high above to meet with . . . a Boy who glowed and burned like nothing I'd ever seen before?

"It's just that you seem different, somehow. The flippancy is still there, that much is clear, but it's like something else is missing. You've changed. How, I do not know."

"News to me, *hombre,*" I said, glancing away from his penetrating stare and folding my arms in cartoon rebellion.

When I looked back, he was stroking his chin in an obvious pantomime of deep thought. After a few seconds and a few more strokes, he shook his head and continued: "The reason I ask, Valentino," he said, also looking away, out, in fact, toward the traffic, "is that it has come to my . . . *our* attention that there might have been . . . how shall I say this? A 'slip' at this location that may have something to do with the current situation."

"'Slip?'" I said, always one for the smart retort. "You've lost me."

"Ah," he said, glee obvious on his French face, "that is the Valentino from before."

Screw you, I thought. "Just tell me," I said with a sigh.

"Perhaps Pogue did not teach you all that was necessary for you to perform your duties? Or maybe it is simply that this information was something you did not understand?"

Before I could say anything, he raised a hand and continued. "Whatever, *mon ami,* that is not important. This," he said, running that same hand down in front of him, as if he were running it down a curtain stitched up with invisible thread, hypothetical fabric, "is what we sense. All that our senses . . . or your senses, for I am aware of a bit more than you are . . . allow us to know. But there is a lot more. Much, much more."

"Keep going, Horatio. I'm following you."

"Witty," Ombre said, pursed lips not showing any kind of amusement. "Shall I continue? Good. There are others that can move between the sheets. Perhaps that is not a good analogy." He must have seen my expression. "They are different . . . have many differences? I don't know how to say. Even most of the *Conseil* cannot fully know them. Their desires and motivations are mostly unknown. They sometimes come, they sometimes cause . . . problems. I have been informed by my superiors that this may have occurred. I have been instructed, and so I am passing those instructions on to you, to be aware of anything that could be considered . . . more unusual."

In San Francisco? Living on the flip side, walking the nighttime twisted streets, the domains of creatures and critters, monsters and monstrosities? Foggy avenues of possibility and potential? Dreams thumbing rides, nightmares passed out in alleys? Werewolf fags and dragulas? Leather-cocooned incubuses unzipping with the dawn into butterfly-winged wet dreams? The foghorn call of suicides? The ringing bell of Clarion summoning lost souls to the cable car to hell?

Julian was dead, drained of life and his precious young years by a faery from the land of shamrocks and green beer. A gang of flavors-of-the-month faeries from the land of JCrew and Tommy Hilfiger caught me, left me to die on some tenement roof? In a building in the Mission District with the cryptic sign of 17 Reasons high above I'd met with . . . a Boy who glowed and burned like nothing I'd ever seen before.

"More unusual?" I said, blinking a few times at what exactly that could mean.

"*Oui,* Monsieur Valentino. That is what I said." He sighed, long and slow and deep. "Please be aware of anything out of the ordinary . . . as you continue with your duties, of course."

"Of course," Polly said, wanting a cracker. "As I continue with my duties."

"That being the pursuit of the rogue vamps, as well as locating our official representative, Mr. Pogue."

"I'll find him—and them. Tell the *Conseil* not to worry their fangs over it."

"*Oui,* their 'fangs.' Do not worry, Monsieur Valentino, I am in contact with *Conseil* and shall inform them of your success, or lack of it, in these matters. If you should require me to assist you, please do not hesitate to ask."

"I won't need your help, Ombre. I have it under control."

"That is evident, yes. But also do be aware of anything out of the ordinary. We are, as yet, unaware of what also may be at work here."

"Got it. Keep an eye out for any 'slips.' Anything else?"

He eyed me as only a dark cloud of velvet and uncertainty could, which I didn't realize until that particular cloud of velvet and uncertainty did. Then: "No, Monsieur Valentino. Nothing else. But I do have one piece of advice, one that I hope you'll accept in the manner it is given."

"Oh, Monsieur? And what is it?"

"Be careful."

And he was gone.

* * *

Standing on a busy street, I was alone. Well, I wasn't, of course, because it was still a busy . . . what night was it? Looking around, I tried to feel it out. Saturday? Nah, it wasn't loud enough, the residents not drunk enough. Monday? No, that couldn't be it; the locals seemed to be in too good a mood. Sunday? Nope, as far as I could see they didn't look like they'd had hellfire and brimstone thundered into their ears.

It didn't matter. It was just something to think about instead of what I should have been thinking about. It was that kind of a night. I was in that kind of a life.

I had things to do. Lots of things to do. I'd walked here, of course, planning on climbing up into 17 Reasons and talking to the glow and fire, the glimmer and shine of The Boy, but I wasn't walking anymore. Instead, I stood on the corner of Latino and Mexican, the slippery spice of their cooking in my nose.

There was something about Ombre, something he'd said. Or what he hadn't said. I didn't know which. I didn't know what. At least not consciously.

Suddenly I wasn't alone on that corner in the Mission District. Mariah came—gliding up out of the night, brights on, motor rumbling—and pulled up to the curb in front of me.

I got in, melting back into the old upholstery, and let him take me away.

XV

"How nice to see you again, officer. I take it you had no troubles with the doorman this time?"

"Yeah, real good to see you too. No, no problem getting in. Guess he's starting to recognize my authority."

"Actually," The Chef said, wiping his bloody hands with a towel, transferring the red stuff to it with a quick dance over and under his fingers, "I told him to let you in if you came back."

"Ah," I said, looking away from him and instead to the body on the examining table. Plump, pudgy, doughy, marked with flank, rump roast, shank, ribs, and other choice cuts. I'd interrupted something as he'd begun to slice along the dotted lines. The red juicy stuff that poured out made me lick my lips and want to scratch my itchy fangs, but I didn't do either and instead just reached out to tweak the corpse's toe. "The special?"

"Oh, my word, no," he said, looking down at the body. "This fellow's hardly up to my standards. I was actually planning on making a nice little stew out of him, use his bones for soup stock. Or . . . you know, I have been thinking of expanding out into a fast- food venue. Maybe he'd make a good experimental burger?"

"Whatever," I said, looking up from his more-than-quarter pounder. "I guess you wanted to talk to me?"

"Indeed," The Chef said, inspecting his fingernails for lingering hemoglobin or much worse. "Have you considered what we discussed earlier? A possible arrangement, I mean?"

"Been a little busy," I said, adding in a "sorry" at the end but not meaning it. At all.

"Pity. I do think some sort of mutually beneficial . . . arrangement, shall we say, would be in both of our best interests. I do have some

The Very Bloody Marys

doi:10.1300/5329_15

rather unique connections in the city, some of which I know could be useful in your work as a representative of the *Conseil.*"

"Could be. But, like I said, I can't really think about that right now. Things are . . . well, things have come up."

"Of course, of course. I understand completely. But let's say, hypothetically, that I might have stumbled across a bit of information that could affect your professional and, quite possibly, your personal life as well. Something that most reasonable people—er, ah 'beings,' for we can't discriminate in our respective lines of work, eh?—would be willing to reward me for, or at least avert their attention from activities that could be considered close to breaking established rules of conduct among our kind."

"Okay," I said, my interest having been piqued. "Hypothetically. Go ahead."

"Excellent. Anyway, hypothetically, what would you imagine information of this sort to be worth to a person such as yourself, in your position as a law enforcement official as well as a member of our underground community?"

"Well, I can't say unless I know what it is."

"Ah, naturally. I understand. Well, the information that I have happened to come across has to do with your superior, our mutual friend, Mr. Pogue. Seems that I served the member of a unique subspecies of hyena that has successfully adapted itself to mimic humanity. This fellow . . . my word, he liked to chat, and was quite complimentary about my veal saltimbocca . . . happened to witness an incident that involved Pogue, the outcome of which, as I said, you might find very interesting."

Four steps was all it took for me to round the stainless-steel table and step up to The Chef. "What do you mean? What did he see?"

"Well, as I initially said, I did think this is something you'd like to know and obviously that's the case. Not to be too bold, but maybe now would be a time to discuss the possibility of a situation between the two of us, one that would work to both of our advantages—"

He didn't finish because what he was about to say stuck in his throat, trapped there by my hand clenched tightly around it. Politically important or not, not hurting humans or not, orders or not, I squeezed until his eyes began to bulge out of their sockets and his face went from pillowcase white to faint then dark blue. "What did you hear?" I growled, the depth and base of my voice sounding like someone else's. Someone even I wouldn't want to meet in a dark alley.

I let go when I realized that, one, he couldn't answer and, two, he was dying. Legs sprawled apart, ass smacking down onto the white tile in a crumble of chef's whites, he sputtered and wheezed, hand massaging his bruised Adam's apple. "Y-you . . ." he squeaked, trying to find his voice.

"Yes, I did. And I'll do it again—and more—if you don't tell me what you know about Pogue."

He found his dignity before he found his voice. Climbing awkwardly to his feet, reclaiming his hat from where it had fallen under the gurney, he adjusted his apron and even went so far as to flick invisible crumbs of humiliation from the front before trying to talk again. "I'll t-tell you, but don't think this won't go unreported to your—"

"Tell me. Right. Now," I said. My mouth felt a bit odd. My fangs, I realized, were bared. It felt odd to have them out. Odd, but good. I wanted to bite him. But more than that, I wanted him to talk.

When his eyes went from my own squinted-in-intimidation pair of peepers to my mouth, and my two front teeth, he shrunk a bit. "I heard . . . I heard that he'd been killed."

"How? What happened?"

"I don't know . . . exactly. I just heard that he was last seen confronting three young vamps. I presumed these were the rogues, naturally. According to my witness they overpowered him, and left him on a rooftop . . . at dawn."

Vanilla, before I blacked out, saying "another." I hadn't thought about that, until now. *My god. Pogue.*

"That's all? What else did he say?"

"Just that . . . he saw Mr. Pogue . . . a bit later in the day."

"And?"

"I said 'day.' He tried to get him down but the sun got him before my witness could. I'm afraid he saw . . . his last moments. I have no reason to doubt him, I'm afraid."

Extending his picking of crumbs off the chest of the corpse on the table, fingers dancing around its hairless nipples, he then seemed to realize how foolish it looked. Reddening, he twisted his neck this way, then that, peering at me with stern chastisement over the pain. "I understand that you and he were not . . . friends, but I understand that this still must be somewhat of a shock. For that you have my—"

He could have said "sympathy," he could have said "pity," he could have said "scorn," or something else entirely, but I'll never know because I had turned and walked out.

Pogue . . . dead?

* * *

Outside, standing in another cool night, I waited for my ride, goose bumps racing up and down my arms.

Standing, yes, shivering, yes, Mariah coming, yes, but I was quiet and still inside, shocked senseless, beaten by news, slammed by information. I didn't want it to be true, desperately didn't want it to be accurate, but it made too much sense.

Pogue was dead.

Sure, I hated him. He was (pick one):

A prick
An asshole
A fucking prick
A fucking asshole
Rude
Crude
Mean
Nasty
Hard-assed
A sergeant in the U.S. Army

When he wasn't ripping me a new one, he was putting his spit-polished boots up my old one. When he wasn't putting me down, he was tearing me up. When he wasn't screaming in my face, he was yelling in my ear.

He treated me like shit, like dirt, like garbage. He thought I was a fool, an idiot, a loser, a failure, a disappointment.

And he was dead. Pogue was dead. Why wasn't I happy about that?

Then I was outside, chilly, and my ride had finally come. But it wasn't Mariah.

* * *

"Val! Yoo-hoo! Over here!" came a voice I knew, from somewhere and something I'd never have expected. Somewhere was out here in the now-foggy, less-blurry, and more distinct part of the city. Something was a van parked by the curb, a battered green thing, all acne of rust and wrinkles of dents. The tires were mismatched and the passenger-side window was fogged with grime. It also sat a bit oddly, leaning far to the left, as if the shocks on that side had been shocked into surrender.

One of the back doors was open, swung wide and hiding the scratchy voice that had reached me across the hum of rushing traffic. In case I hadn't noticed where it had come from, the owner of the voice also waved a cane, a bobbing metronome keeping time with every syllable.

"Saul?" I said when I followed the voice and the cane, walking around to the back of the van.

"Climb up, Val. Sit your ass down right here next to me and we'll get going."

"Wait a minute. What's going on?"

"You mean my little mobile home? Have a seat and I'll tell you all about it."

His wheelchair was wedged tightly in the back, his frizzled white head only an inch or so from the roof of the van. Next to him was a scratchy wool blanket, folded neatly. I climbed in, twisting myself this way and that until my back was against the side of the van and my feet were gently resting against his left wheel.

With a nimbleness I didn't think he had, Saul leaned forward and hooked the open door with the crook of his cane and, with a quick jerk, swung it shut. I heard the engine cough to grumbling, grinding life and we almost immediately lurched into traffic.

I caught myself from falling by reaching out, bracing myself against the filthy side panel, feeling grime crumble under my fingertips. Considering he was a bronze statue, Abe wasn't a bad driver. It also explained the shot shocks on that side. Ford never intended its drivers to weigh just short of half a ton.

"So, you holding up okay?" Saul said, wrinkled face only partially revealed as slices of light scrolled through the dark interior of the van.

I shrugged, then realized that if he hadn't passed some neon signs or driven past headlights he might not have seen the gesture. "I've had better days," I commented.

"Poor boychick," the wizard said, voice scratchy and immeasurably old but also warm, comforting. Saul. My friend Saul. My good friend Saul. "It has been quite a trial for you, eh?"

"So what's up with the van? I thought the wizard was supposed to have people come to him? Yellow-brick road and all that?"

It took him a minute to answer, like he was trying to pick the right words. "What, an old man can't drive around and get some air? What am I supposed to be, a mushroom?"

"Saul . . . why the wheels?"

"Okay, okay; I'll tell. You know how things have been of late, what with the vamps and weird things and all. I just thought it might be a good idea to maybe get a bit more mobile, you know. Get myself out of that stuffy place and get some fresh air."

"Sorry, Saul. I ain't buying it."

"What, do I look like a liar?" A slow breath then, a whistle in, a moan out. "Okay, okay, it's like this. I threw down some chicken bones last night, you know, scatter some on a Monopoly board and pick up a chance? Didn't look good, Val. Didn't look good at all. Now I'm not complaining. I'm not that kind of a fella, but I'll tell ya, once I saw the way those things fell, I thought that it might be time to move around a bit. Become less of a target."

"I'm sorry, Saul. You lost me."

"Something's happening, Val. Something my Aunt Xena would say is 'Vot good. Bery vot good.' Poor Xena," he added, voice fading as he remembered what happened to yet another member of his extended and witchy lineage. "I didn't just throw the bones, Val. I also threw some Scrabble tiles in some soup—not as good as Uncle Filo could do but if I do say so myself not half bad—and spooned them out. 'Vot good' portents there. Then I blew on the Torah, reading backwards the pages that moved in a mirror. Then I put a little green lizard in a jar, shook him up good and let him loose. Little bastard ran right up to the tip of my nose. That's what did it, son. So I decided to get out for a while." The van must have driven down Geary, through the theater district, because for a moment the interior was bright and clear. Saul was in his chair, still turned toward the back, but he was looking right at me, his blue eyes gleaming long after the lights had passed by. "There's something out there, Val. Something you don't want to meet."

"I heard. My *Conseil* contact said that, too, about a 'slippage,' or something. Said to keep my eyes out for anything weird."

Saul snorted, his laughter worn away by the years to something like a coughing fit. "Like that's easy to do in this place? Eh, but he's right; from here it probably isn't. It doesn't feel like a local kind of thing. You . . . uh, notice anything, Val?"

"Me? No. Not really." And that was true. It was all terrifying, but none of it really felt out of place. The rogue vamps, Julian dying, The Boy, Pogue—all perfectly part of my usual nighttime landscape. Or that's the way it felt. Pogue. . . . "He's dead," I heard myself mumble to myself.

For a thousand years old, he had damned good hearing. "I heard, Val. Sorry."

Hearing that he'd heard but hadn't said anything made my eyebrows knit and my heart beat faster. "When, Saul? You didn't tell me?" My good friend Saul. Maybe.

"Val, Val, Val, would I not tell you something like that? What do I look like to you? I heard a few hours ago. The Pigeon King told me, in exchange for some nice challah. Saw the whole thing, he did, when he was making his royal rounds. Said that Pogue was a crazy-man, going after those vamps on his own. Not like him, you know. The man was a putz but not a dumb one. Like it was personal or something."

Damn, the wrinkled old wiz was right. He was. It shut me up. Why would Pogue go after the Marys on his own? Okay, he thought I was as helpful as tits on a bull but he wouldn't have just gone tearing after three fresh vamps without some kind of backup. Something was seriously weird about that.

"Do you think this weirdness got to him?"

"Who knows? Maybe, maybe not. What am I, perfect or something? The man was wound up a bit too tight; maybe he just had a fit. If he was still here, I could take a look, but the good man's not." With that he brought a pale hand up, curled it into a tube, and looked through it at me again. Through the circle I could see one of his too-blue eyes, blinking, blinking, blinking, blinking. "What about you, son? How are you dealing with all this? Feeling okay?"

"I—" I began to say but stopped. How the hell did I feel? The rogue vamps, Julian dying, The Boy, Pogue. . . . I might have been riding in an ancient piece of Detroit mechanics but I felt like I'd been standing in the road and flattened by its pockmarked-chrome and bug-graveyard grill. Roll me up, stick me in the ground, and cover my immortal bod with soft peat. I was done.

"I don't know," I said, sort of lying, sort of telling the truth. Yeah, I wanted to crawl into a hole somewhere and pull the dirt over me, but I also had a job to do. For Julian, for me, and not for that asshole, bastard, cocksucker, prick . . . Pogue.

I looked toward the front of the truck, trying to judge the hour. It was a good way to cover my exhaustion and confusion. "I should be getting home, Saul."

"Of course, son. Of course. Abe's been getting us there. Don't think I'd like my favorite vamp to turn to dust now, do you? You get yourself some rest, a little nosh maybe—'cause if you don't mind me saying so you're looking a little on the skin-and-bones side—and rest up. Me? Abe here will drive me around and I'll keep these tired old eyes open for anything unusual. You do the same?"

"Of course, Saul. Of course." Sure enough, through the narrow glimpse of windshield, I saw a few bright-light landmarks of my neighborhood. Home again, home again. Even though the thought of my apartment instantly brought up the blunt-edged trauma weapon of Julian's dust at the foot of my bed, the thought of the bed itself mattered more. That and the blood ordinary in the fridge; my eyes might have been tired but my stomach was growling like a lion poked with a sharp stick.

Saul popped the back door, again with a masterful bit of cane twirling, and I crawled out. But before Abe drove him off into the slowly dying night, I put my hand on the door. "Saul?"

"Yes, Val? What is it? Something you want to tell me?"

"Just that—well, thanks, Saul. For everything."

"Oh, that. Got to stick together, don't we?" But before I could close the door, or he and his statue could drive away, he also asked: "Val?"

"Yes, Saul?"

"I know that Julian's . . . passing . . . was hard on you, but try not to be a prick about it, okay? Try to think about what Pogue would do. Not what he did, though. You know what I mean, right?"

I didn't, but my lion was being poked more and my eyes felt like they'd been buried in sand. "I know what you mean, Saul. I know exactly what you mean."

XVI

As the van with Saul (behind Abe) and Abe (behind the wheel) pulled away, screeching and careening out onto Castro Street, I watched them go, not thinking much of anything . . . except maybe one of the following:

I'm tired.
I'm hungry.

Key out, I made my way across the sidewalk to my secret little door, already envisioning climbing the narrow stairs, heading into the kitchen, opening the fridge, pouring myself a shot of average-ordinary-bland blood, knocking it back—even bypassing my traditional vodka in my rush to fill my belly—and then to bed, crawling between the sheets, all the time trying not to notice the pile of dust and ash at the foot. The dust and ash that had been Julian. The love of my life.

The love of my life. Yes, the love of my life. That was Julian, and he was dead.

But . . . ashes and dust at the foot of my bed. It seemed like a century ago I'd seen him crumble to nothing. The memory felt strange, like I'd replayed it too many times or something, my brain wearing the tape thin.

My key skated around the lock. *More tired than I thought,* I thought. Then a sound, a special kind of sound, and I fumbled with the keys, almost dropping them.

Take a bee and make it huge. Take a bunch of "e"s in a single scream. Take a huge balloon and rub it until it screeches. It was a four-stroke sound, a small cc sound, a foreign sound, an imported sound, a sporty sound, a two-wheeled sound.

The Very Bloody Marys

doi:10.1300/5329_16

But that wasn't quite right, because it wasn't just one sound—singular—but instead, better yet, three bees, three sets of "e"s, three balloons. Three of them, like Father, Son, and Holy Ghost. Like Good, Bad, and Ugly. Like Moe, Larry, and Curly. Like Heaven, Limbo, and . . . Hell.

Or Chocolate, Green Tea, and Vanilla.

Thank god for those sounds. Had the characters been on foot, instead of on their wheels, I might not have heard them coming. Luckily I did, so I did what I did, which was duck.

Ducking is good. Ducking is very good—especially since one of the vamps had a golf club and as he sped toward me, he swung, the metal of his five iron ringing with a slash of contrasting metals when it hit my head, just about where I'd been standing.

Fuck, I thought. *Fuck, fuck, fuck.*

Chocolate had swung and missed, roaring by and down the sidewalk, scattering queens and leather daddies in his wake like macho and femmie tenpins. A few of them threw harsh words at his stylish back after he'd passed, but looking back toward where he'd come from, they ducked for better cover.

Grateful for their early warning, so did I. The next one, Green Tea, was on another bike, and he had a chain this time. As I dove away from my door, aiming for a gap between two parked cars, the chain spun out of the night; a glimmering guillotine, tearing a jagged scar into a delicate paint job, sparking and scratching as it ruined.

Crap, I thought. *Oh, crap.*

On the other side of my safe little gap was rushing evening traffic, tons of impatient metal trying to get somewhere—anywhere—fast. Getting across would be difficult, if not impossible.

"So the drama!" screamed the last fag, his imported wheels cutting right by my head. Ducking back, I sprawled on my ass between a front and a back bumper.

Shit, I thought. *Shit, shit, shit.*

Déjà vu and déjà vu again. I had the same choice I had before, an option that was a familiar bolt of lightning between my ears. Stay and get killed by these hissing vamps or get the hell out of there; try to ditch them somehow.

So I ran. Again. I just hoped it would work out better this time.

* * *

One foot in front of the other, nothing but running, nothing but panic. Breath hot and quick in and out, legs burning, then transforming into lead. Heart knocking heavy, urgently, in my chest.

Cars blasted past, leaving around me as I ran, horns and screaming profanity marking their arrival, taillights signs of their leaving.

I darted left, ducked right when I thought of it, and also when I heard anything that sounded like the four-stroke buzz of a scooter. Sparks from near misses with the five iron, sparks from near misses with the chain. I didn't know where I was, or where I was going, or anything, except for the very, very basics: I was in trouble, and needed to be anywhere but here—where the trouble was.

Between the many moments of panic, I tried to think. I had to do something, and quick. Damned quick. The twinks were playing with me; that much was clear. The instant I started to really slow down or they got bored with their little game I would become toasted undead. I doubted they'd go to the trouble of leaving me to bake on a rooftop again.

A scooter cut in front of me, narrow tires screaming on the pavement. On it was Green Tea, and in Green Tea's hand was the five iron, which he swung straight at my head.

I jumped back, reflexively baring my fangs. I wanted to reach out, grab his slender little neck. I might have even tried—I was either that pissed off or had gone that far around the bend—but an additional screech of tires made me dart in a new, and cowardly, direction.

"I missed you!" said Chocolate from his set of wheels as his chain swung toward my head. I'd already begun my strategic withdrawal down a narrow alley.

Narrow for a car, maybe, but not for someone on foot, and not for Vespas. I had a second, maybe two, before the Marys followed.

Okay, less than a second. "I'm coming, darling!" shrilled one of them from behind me as a headlight pinned my silhouette to a moldy brick wall. Running became sprinting, sprinting led to tripping, tripping led to falling, falling could have led to dying.

But then his wheels hit some bottles, cans, or other noisy debris and the Mary twisted, handlebars grinding a discordant clash back and forth against the alley walls. The headlight flashed and wove, turning my piss-reeking escape path into an impromptu disco. I wasn't sure if he had completely crashed, but I sure as hell didn't stick around to find out.

I was out the other end of the alley in a flash—bounding, leaping, running just like the little white rabbit I felt I was.

* * *

"See ya! Wouldn't wanna be ya!"

"Love handles come with baggage, girlfriend!"

"Lookit that bitch run!"

I needed help. No shit, Sherlock.

"You go, girl!"

"This time we ain't gonna tan ya, we's gonna eat ya!"

"I'm working up an appetite here!"

The Chef wouldn't help anyone, ever, unless he was getting something out of it. Hell, I wouldn't put it past him to have a well-manicured hand in some of this. Get rid of one cop, then his fucked-up trainee. Have the city all to himself. But that was for later. Right now, the important thing was running.

"Lookit that ass—and his rear's not too bad, either!"

"Can we lick you?"

"Kissy-kissy-kissy!"

Saul was powerful in a very scary way, but he was also older than sin and as fragile as a promise. He was also in a van, being driven around by a bronze statue of Abraham Lincoln, and I had no idea where either of them was.

"Sugar's good enough to eat!"

"I'm licking my lips!"

"If we catch ya, can we keep ya?"

Julian was there, in my mind, woven through my memories. A pleasant, ideal ghost. Here with a smile, there with a helping hand; here with a kiss, there with love. He was there—but he wasn't here.

"I love it when they run; their blood gets so *hot*!"

"I'm getting hungry, girls."

"Let's have a bite!"

Pogue. . . . He was dead. Gone. They'd killed him.

What would Pogue do?

* * *

"You pathetic excuse for an undead bloodsucker! You call yourself a . . . well, son, I can't see how you can call yourself anything but a fucking failure!"

Where the hell was I? Confusion and exhaustion made my head swim—the backstroke, if you must know. If you don't need to know, well, then all you need to hear is one word: Lost.

But *where* was less important than *why*. For that, three reasons remained: Chocolate, Vanilla, and Green Tea. They didn't seem to care where we were either; they just wanted me dead. Still.

So I kept running. But while I was running I was also trying to think. Desperately trying to think.

"Repeat after me, you no-account, worthless piece of vampiric filth! To defeat your enemy, you must understand your enemy! Do we have agreement on this, you miserable bastard? What did you say? *I can't hear you!*"

Polished links gleamed out of the night, caught in a streetlight's cone of harsh light. I jumped back, but not fast enough. Something burned my arm, something ripped into my arm, something cut my arm, something hurt like a fucking sonofabitch. Green Tea smiled as he sped past on his scooter, the familiar aroma of my own blood twirling away on his chain.

First blood: the Marys. First and maybe final. If I didn't think of something first.

"Listen up, you stinking pile of shit! Are you listening? You don't fucking *look* like you're listening! Do I finally have your *fucking* attention? Good! Now listen up, you greasy smear of a used-to-be-a-man. When faced by overwhelming adversaries one should do the unexpected. This may very well buy you sufficient time to regroup or plan a counterattack. Is this getting through, you useless asshole? *Is it?*"

My arm was hurt—hurt bad. Hurt damned bad. Hurt really bad. I could feel, through the ache, the pain, a lot of blood dripping from the gash. I didn't check it out though; stopping for even an instant was too much of a risk. So I kept running, hoping that something would come to me. Anything.

"You paying attention, maggot? *Are you paying attention?!* Stand straight, for Christ's sake! At least pretend to have a fucking backbone! Another way to oppose superior forces—of a natural or unnatural variety—is to use their own tactics against them. *Do I make myself clear?!*"

Chocolate was approaching me from behind. I was starting to recognize the roar and throaty bellow of their individual motors. *Vroom* was Green Tea. *Meeeerrrr* was Vanilla. *Peeeer* was what was getting louder and louder and *louder,* and it was Chocolate.

After Green Tea's swing with the chain, I'd bolted back toward the sidewalk from where I'd been trying to lose them in late-night traffic. Chocolate had jumped the curb far behind, just in case I did exactly that.

Chocolate had the golf club.

Ahead was a corner, the meeting of avenues . . . or streets . . . or boulevards. I didn't know or care. All I saw were two things. The first was a sturdy metal pole on the corner, an anchor for a streetlight . . . a stoplight . . . a power pole for a streetcar. I didn't know or care. All I saw was a study in metal.

I ran up to it, putting what I hoped was enough distance between the Mary and that sturdy metal. Once there, I spun around to face him. I thought for a second of trying to look scared and panicked but then realized I didn't need to do any acting.

There he was, screaming toward me on two important wheels, eyes bright and eager for the sight of my skull cracking open and my brains flying like thrown oatmeal.

Then I ducked, and five iron met sturdy metal pole with a *clang* and a *clash* and, more importantly, a clear, sharp, *snap*. Swerving, trying to maintain his balance on his scooter, the Mary squealed out a very satisfying *"Fuck!"* as the golf club snapped in two. One Mary minus one weapon. Hardly a victory but I'd take what I could get.

The other thing I noticed as I took a quick second to catch my breath—the *Vroom* of Green Tea, the *Meeeerrrr* of Vanilla, the *Peeeer* of Chocolate in front of me for once—was that the pole wasn't a streetlight, a stoplight, or a power pole. It was a street sign, and more importantly, I recognized the street. I knew where I was.

Suddenly, against all odds, I had an idea. Pogue would have been proud. Well, maybe he would have been. No, mostly he would have been pissed that it had taken me this long to think of it.

Now all I had to do was pull it off without getting killed.

* * *

So I ran, but this time I had a direction (aside from the general idea of *away*). With all three Marys in front of me, it gave me a second or two's lead on them—a lead I hoped they were smart enough, or dumb enough, to follow. After a few burning strides, I realized they were. I just hoped it had been the latter and not the former.

A few blocks. That's all I had to go. A few blocks with one armed and two unarmed tweaking fags on Vespas. No, I wouldn't have put money on me making it, either.

"Move it, move it, *move it,* you pathetic pile of stinking shit! My *fucking* grandmother could run faster than you!"

Sir, yes, sir!

I could hear them coming. Their banter had died away, replaced by simple growls and screams of fury, so I knew the game was getting old for them. Play was one thing, but for their prey to have lived this long was getting to be more of an insult. Might as well make it even more so.

I had about a ten-second lead, ten seconds I could afford to blow to get them too mad to think about where they were heading. Spinning around, my eyes caught them at the bottom of the hill I'd been running up. Green Tea, Chocolate, and Vanilla rounding the distant corner, heading toward me with revving engines and dazzling headlights.

"Hey, you fucking faggots!" I yelled. "You worthless pieces of undead crap! Yeah, I'm talking to *you*!"

Pogue would not have been impressed with the impersonation, but the message was definitely delivered. The instant I started to scream at them, their engines throttled up and their narrow tires bit the road hard with screaming rubber.

I finished with, "Kiss my fucking ass!" A classic. Just in case they couldn't hear me, I spanked myself and leered back at their brilliant glares.

That did it. Oh, boy, that did it. Even over their *Vrooms, Meeeerrrrs,* and *Peeers,* I could hear their bellows of rage.

One block to go. I almost didn't make it. Legs burning, filled with blistering lead, lungs blistered, throat scarred, I pushed and pushed and pushed myself more and more and more.

"*Move it,* you stinking piece of fucking shit! *Move it!*"

But I had legs, lungs, and throat—not imported machinery. Naturally, they caught up to me. Two addresses from the building, their *Vrooms, Meeeerrrrs,* and *Peeers* were right *there* in my ears, and I knew I had to do something, and quick.

So I did. *Sir, yes, sir, I understand about doing the unexpected. Yes, indeedy, sir!*

I spun and ran back toward them. Oh, you should have seen their faces. Actually, I wish you had because you could tell me if what I saw was what I saw: delightful panic, cherished fear, wonderful shock on their prissy little queenie faces. Scooters one, two, and three (Chocolate, Green Tea, and Vanilla) jerked this way, that way, and that-a-way. One into the side of a building, two others into parked cars.

Three crashes. Music to my ears.

For a second, I thought about trying to take them out while they were topsied and turvied, smacked and dazed, banged and bruised, tipped and toppled, but then I realized that it would still be three against one.

Besides, I had a plan.

"Hey, Marys!" I yelled at their groaning but already standing and growling forms. "Suck this!" This time it wasn't my ass that got pulled into play. Cupping my dick, I gave them all the goombah salute. *Kind of appropriate,* I thought.

Then I turned and ran the last few feet up to my destination. The last time I was here, the door was crappy, just like the rest of the building, and hadn't closed right.

Sure enough, when I hit it, the thing popped right open. Thank goodness the landlord was cheap and/or lazy. If I got through this, I'd have to send him something nice. Flowers, maybe. Or a box of candy.

I was about to turn around to make sure the Marys were still on my tail but just as I hit the first stair, I heard them crash through the door as well, their rumblings and roarings bouncing back and forth off the cheap plaster walls.

This would be tricky. The timing had to be perfect. I had to get one floor ahead of them, be out of their sight for at least a few seconds for this to work. Again, I thought about Pogue; about how much of a help he'd been—in this situation and at other times as well, even though I really didn't want to admit it.

But then I remembered that he was dead. I worried, for a second, that I would need a miracle to be able to do something he couldn't: kill the Bloody Marys. It also made me angry, for a second. Furious for another second. Blind with rage for a further second.

Why, I didn't know. At least not yet.

So far, so good. One more floor, the sounds of their pursuit right behind me. Two pairs of feet pounding up step after step, to the top.

Then I was there. *Come on,* I thought. *Come on! Move it, you undead sack of shit!* The door handle was in my hand, the door was open.

Then they rounded the last flight. I knew what they'd see, could picture it perfectly: Steps going up to an open door. Beyond it the roof. The same roof they'd left me on. The same roof they used to kill Pogue. Who knew what they thought? Maybe they bared their fangs in memory. Maybe they appreciated the irony of my picking this place to run to. I just hoped they didn't think too much.

I know what *I* thought: that Pogue, wherever he was, might have smiled as they rushed up onto the roof. He might have grinned, just a little bit, as they looked around, trying to find me but not succeeding. He might even have laughed, that deep guffaw he'd sometimes let loose when something tickled the single sensitive part of his solid-brass soul, when I did what I hoped I'd be able to do.

Simple, sweet, and very satisfying. I hid behind the door. When they ran by, I simply closed it behind them, trapping them on their own roof.

And dawn was due in less than an hour.

XVII

Have you ever had your life turned upside down?

Not just upside down, not just a simple inversion, but rather shaken, stirred, whipped, frothed, churned, mixed, blended, frappéed, tossed, and agitated?

This hadn't just become *that*; *this* had become a very backwards *siht*. The moon had come up with the dawn, and at dusk the sun came out. Grass was red, water was yellow, blood was blue, the sky was plaid, and fire was paisley. The world wasn't what it had been.

Nothing was what it had been.

I was walking. My name is Valentino. I am a vampire, and I was walking.

Where was I walking? Not knowing, I stopped. Night. It was night, and I'd been walking. I, the vampire named Valentino, had been walking, but then I'd stopped.

The moon was full, the sky dusted with stars. I blinked, making sure the colors and position were right. They were. It was me that was different.

The vampire named Valentino. That was what was different.

* * *

I'd killed. I know how silly that sounds—a vampire named Valentino in shock after killing someone—and you are right; it was silly, because even though I'd killed, and killed, and killed (to be technical), that wasn't why the world was twisted, knotted, folded, creased, and flipped.

Hard to believe that after all these nights on Earth, with all that had happened with me, I'd killed only a few times. Chicago, of course; that loss of hot-blooded virginity. A few times after. Only in desperation, I'd justified. Only when threatened, I'd rationalized.

The Very Bloody Marys

doi:10.1300/5329_17

One or two, here and there. But where I was now was very different from here and there. This was the world of backwards, of sideways, of inversion, of convolution.

Here I'd killed three people in the space of a few hours. A few daylight hours.

Chocolate, Green Tea, and Vanilla. Ashes to ashes, dust to dust, blowing off a rooftop, particles of bad vamps mixing with general air pollution. Now just a scratchy throat, one or two attack coughs, then nothing else.

I don't even know which one went first. To me they'd been just three young twinks on scooters, complete with catcalls and revving motors. I hadn't had the time to fix any of their voices to their faces.

But one had gone first. And then there were two.

Door shut behind them, dawn rising fast, it hadn't taken them very long to realize where they were, what had happened, and what was going to happen very soon.

They'd tried the knob, but I'd locked it. Then they banged on the door. Fists pounding (drums and thunder to me on the other side), shrieking in fury and then in fear, they tried to batter or threaten it open.

But I'd locked it. Or have I already said that?

The old lady had come, perhaps the only one who'd heard or the only one with any interest, or any conscience, to check. I'd bared my fangs at her, growled low in my throat, and told her to go away.

She did, cowering and whimpering, fist pressed to her lips.

The threats went on for a long time. Some I'd heard before. Others were new. None of them frightened me enough to cause me to think of opening the door, letting them into the darkness and away from the looming sunrise.

Then the pleading started. Some of the cries I'd heard before. Others were new. Some of them, like when they screamed in terror, made my hand go to the knob, but I didn't turn it. Even when the sunrise wasn't just looming.

At first there were three screeching, hissing, caterwauling voices, raging at what they would do to me, to my mother, to various components of my body. Then there were three screeching, hissing, caterwauling voices whimpering for my sympathy, pledging the turning over of new leaves, or loyal servitude.

Then there were only two voices, both of them beginning with a duet of terror, then fading down to syncopated tears of sorrow. It took me a moment to realize that one of them—I don't know which flavor—had jumped off the roof.

While they pleaded, they also offered apologies. To me, for chasing me, for hitting me with golf clubs, for cutting my arm with a chain, for leaving me to die on the roof, for hurting me in any way.

Then they apologized for their victims. Men they'd winked and battered long eyelashes at. Men they'd sashayed for and lured into alleys. Men they'd minced into darkened rooms. Men they'd bitten, throats they'd chewed, blood they'd drunk, bodies they'd left to rot or rolled into the bay.

This went on for quite a while. They'd been busy.

Luckily, I noted, they seemed to have a pretty good grasp of how things worked. When they bit, they killed them, sucking all of them until they were pale and dry. They liked their exclusive club of three.

Then they'd gone on to other apologies, spoke of other men they'd simply killed because they could, or whimsically wanted to. Bullies and bashers they'd torn apart, ugly trolls they'd crushed under the wheels of their Vespas.

Then they'd mentioned a different vamp, the first one they'd dragged up to this roof to see the view. They said he'd been a good fighter, better than any of them. He'd almost gotten them, in fact; would have if there hadn't been three of their flavors to one of his.

Then, at the end of this apology, they said something else. Something that made it all turn over. That changed *this* not just into *that,* but *this* into a very backwards *siht*. The moon had come up with the dawn, at dusk the sun came out. Grass was red, water was yellow, blood was blue, the sky was plaid, and fire was paisley.

No, no, no: That wasn't it. That wasn't it at all. The world was the same. I was the one who'd changed, who had become different.

All because of what Pogue had said as he'd attacked them.

* * *

Standing. I was standing. It was night and I was standing. Standing on the sidewalk.

Then, standing, still standing, my stomach had growled, and I realized I had a place to go. And so I began to walk.

One step, two steps. Three steps, four. Down the street. I was hungry. Very hungry. I needed to eat.

I had a destination. It was something, at least. A *there* to add to my *here*. I forced myself to take stock of myself, not to fall backwards into my own mind. I seemed to be okay. Where the one Mary's chain had bitten my arm, there was now nothing but a dull, throbbing ache. A little blood and some rest and I should be ready to face the next night.

I was a sight. I had the sidewalk to myself; everyone I passed crossing the street tossed frightened glances over their shoulders at me. I didn't mind. I was heading home. Home was not only a glass or two of blood but also a shower and my bed.

That there was probably dust or grit at the base of my bed didn't bother me. Not like it used to.

A red light and the little man saying DON'T WALK stopped me at one corner. I rasped and wheezed in a steadying breath. My pulse was pounding, jiggling my vision of the cars streaking by. A few more rasps, a few more wheezes, and the jiggling slowed, then stopped.

Not far now. Just a dozen or so blocks to the Castro, and my windowless little box, my home, and rest.

Back to my life. My life without Julian.

The name, even just thinking it in the empty coconut of my head, still managed to give me a running shiver from one shoulder to the other, making me raise them both. I stopped again, closing my eyes, trying to block out the sound of traffic rushing by, the footsteps of my fellow pedestrians, music leaking from glowing windows or spilling from storefronts, and repeated the name over and over again in my mind:

Julian (shudder) *Julian* (shudder) *Julian* (shudder) *Julian* (shudder) *Julian* (shudder) *Julian* (shudder) *Julian* (shudder) *Julian* (shudder) *Julian* (shudder) *Julian* (shudder).

But then, as I thought it (over and over and over) the shudder began to fade, the shiver wore off, my shoulders stopped rising.

Julian (nothing) *Julian* (nothing) *Julian* (nothing) *Julian* (nothing) *Julian* (nothing) *Julian* (nothing) *Julian* (nothing).

Opening my eyes, taking in another calming breath, I thought his name one last time, just to make sure.

Julian (nothing).

It was good, and so I smiled. Good that his name meant nothing. Because, as I had found out, Julian had been nothing to begin with.

* * *

Home again, home again, jiggity jog. The Castro was quiet tonight; odd, but also, in a strange way, comforting. I don't know what would have happened to my mind as I walked up to The Midnight Sun, fed my brass key into my hungry lock, and turned, hearing a fast, lively, happy Castro around me: friendly voices chirping and sparking, hands being held, kisses being given, promises made, hearts going a-twitter.

A quiet night was what I needed and what I got: a contemplative evening of low voices, whispered hopes, gentle conversations.

Up the stairs next, one step after another. Even though I was filthy, starving, and exhausted I took them singularly, not bounding or leaping up. A contemplative night, all right, a cool and well-paced night. One meant for deep thoughts and careful considerations.

And powerful revelations.

I should have realized it. I should have seen what had happened. But with the guilt, I shook my head, even though there was no one in my place to see it. No. There was no way I could have. That was the point. That was how it worked. I hadn't seen it. Pogue hadn't seen it.

Saul had, I realized. That explained the bizarre way he'd spoken to me, both in his van and his also-moving apartment in the hazy fog zone of the Sunset. The wizard couldn't tell me what he knew because I wouldn't have believed him. I hadn't been myself. The only thing he could do was watch me, hoping I'd do what I just did.

That I'd snap out of it.

I didn't bother with the vodka. Down went straight, cheap blood in a shot glass. One. Two. Three. Four. Oh, man, that was good. Salty, coppery, sweet, and enriching. I could feel it pour into my empty belly, each drop a thump, thump, thump of relief. Blood: it does a body good.

Shoes off next; then the shirt, the pants, the undies. Naked, I stretched, listening to the bones groan, my spine snap. It felt good, not to be possessed. Not exactly relaxing, because there was still a joint or two or three or four that was still knotted with responsibility, but I felt better than I had in days.

A shower. Then bed. Then . . . tomorrow. Into the bathroom (a shudder, then, but not because of Julian—man, I lived like a pig), and then the stall. A twist of one for hot, a twist of the other for cold until it was like the bear's porridge. Then under the pounding spray. Blood and dust and dirt and sweat running down my legs and then around and around before vanishing down the drain.

Tomorrow, yeah. Tomorrow a trip to the Mission, a journey to 17 Reasons, to have a meeting with The Boy. I didn't know what I'd do after that.

The Boy. I stopped lathering my pits and pressed them, still slippery, on the tile, forcing my face into the spray. The jets bit into my lips, stabbed my lids. The Boy.

Thinking of The Boy reminded me of Pogue. Thinking of Pogue didn't make me shudder; it made me curl one hand into a fist, pound the shower stall wall until I thought the small bones would break.

Pogue (pound) *Pogue* (pound) *Pogue* (pound) *Pogue* (pound) *Pogue* (pound) *Pogue* (pound) *Pogue* (pound) *Pogue* (pound) *Pogue* (pound).

He was gone. He was dead. Killed trying to take on three rogue vamps all on his lonesome. That hurt, but I didn't know why. All I knew was that it did. A lot.

Julian didn't. Where he had been in my life, there was nothing. He was gone. But then he hadn't been there to begin with.

It was a tricky way to do it. Way too complicated, but then, as Pogue liked to say: "You listening to me, you vampiric turd? Are you comp-re-hending me? Things here don't work in fucking straight lines. You think that way and you're going to get your fucking head fucking chopped off. Things out here are twisted. Fucking twisted. Got that? You understand me?"

Sir, yes, sir.

Want to cause chaos and disorder? Want to take down the local authority? Want to clear the playing field?

Give them what they want. A perfect friend. A perfect lover. A dream. A fantasy. Give them what they always wanted.

Then take it away. Murder it—and point the finger at someone else. Julian was mine, killed supposedly by Liam of the faeries, who I was then supposed to kill in revenge.

But Julian had been a trick, a trap, a dream, a bit of animated thought, a lure with blue eyes, a bushwhack with perfect pecs.

It took losing Pogue for me to see that. It took hearing what he'd said, just before the Marys got him, that made me open my eyes, made Julian fade away, made me become nothing but shame and fury at having been used.

Out of the shower, I dried off with a towel I knew was stiff and dirty but tried not to think about exactly how stiff and dirty. In my foggy mirror over the sink I looked at my arm, winced at the healing gash, decided it didn't need anything but my blood-sucky physiology to heal up. Then, naked, I padded out of the bathroom and into the bedroom.

At the foot of my bed . . . nothing. No dust, no ashes, no remains, no specks of bone. Just like he'd never been here. Which, of course, he hadn't.

Into bed, then. Sheets up to my neck, turning to the side (always the right), and closing my eyes, trying to let sleep completely catch up to and swallow me.

Trying . . . because despite the weight of exhaustion in my bones, the flopping of wrung-out muscles attached to them, the lead in my eyelids, sleep danced around, always out of reach, sticking out its tongue and going nah-nah-nah.

Because something was still bothering me. Pogue. He was bothering me. I knew now why he went, against all reason (especially his), up against three—count them, three—bad vamps. I knew what had happened to my boss to make him go all crazy in the head.

I knew it because one of the Marys had confessed it, as part of his last apology to try to get me to open that door. The last thing they'd said as the sun had come up, their screams and pleas ending with twin roars of combustion as their bodies met daylight, transforming them into charcoal and windblown ash.

They said that as Pogue had torn into them he'd yelled "For The Boy!"

That's what had done it for me, what had turned my world upside down—and shaken, stirred, whipped, frothed, churned, mixed, blended, frappéed, tossed, and agitated it. That's what had made me open my eyes and not see Julian, or see him for what he was. Which was nothing.

What I didn't know, and what kept me awake, was one question:

Who was it that Pogue thought he'd lost?

XVIII

It was a dust kinda town, a howling wind kinda town. It was a place of swinging doors, rolling tumbleweeds, and dogs looking for places to die. It was a used-up place, a place thrown away and forgotten. It was a mean kinda place, where everything else had been boiled away by a mean sun and meaner men, leaving behind their cracked bones and their toothless grins. It was Hell. A town called Hell.

Then he came into town: A hard man, a man all tough and gristle. A man who dealt death, lightning with his triggers. A man with no name (waa-waa-waa).

They watched him ride in, the dried-up men of Hell. They watched him with eyes of glass and fists of tough leather. Some looked and thought about trying to take him, to draw their own and squeeze, bullets cracking through the stale air, to drop his blood on the ground.

Others hoped they would draw, they would fire at the Stranger, 'cause, when they did and he dropped them before their iron could come free of their holsters, these more clever beasts would turn on them before their blood had dried in the sun, picking them clean of anything to sell, anything to use, anything to eat.

(waa-waa-waa)

Nah, no one does Westerns anymore. Besides, I'd had a shower, I had a name, and the city was cold and faintly wet from a late-night mist. I might have *felt* like Clint, like Oaks, like Coburn, like Bronson, like Cleif, like Fonda, like Wayne, like Scott, but nothing else was co-operating.

But that didn't stop me from striding down 18th Street from The Midnight Sun. It didn't stop me from putting Clint's glare into my blues, or Oaks's swagger into my legs, Coburn's cocky grin on my lips, Bronson's cement-mixer tones into my throat, Cleif's mean-ass attitude into mine, Fonda's righteous fury mixed with my own, Wayne's laid-back strength into my swinging shoulders, or Scott's firm chin

The Very Bloody Marys

doi:10.1300/5329_18

onto my own clenched jaw. I didn't know if I looked like any of those tough cowboys or a prissy queen trying to butch it up.

I didn't know or really care. I had something else on my mind. I had somewhere important to go—and someone to kill.

Maybe that was the right way to look at it.

I am vengeance.

Gotham. A city of old brick and crumbling iron; as dark, as twisted, as are the thieves, weighing the innocent for the coins in their pockets. The bosses, fat from the lives they'd destroyed. The killers, knives gleaming with the faces of victims. The insane, happy with the horror of it all. And men . . . men with guns.

They wait, in the shadows, for the good men, honest men, women, children, families, to walk by. They reach out, try to take everything from them: money, life, hope, love, leaving behind nothing but bodies and blood on the cold stone streets.

I am the night.

But they're afraid, because they know they are not alone in the dark. There's something else in there with them. Something more terrifying than their knives, their fists, their guns. It is more unstoppable, relentless, unforgiving, and terrifying than they could ever be.

Me.

I am—

No, that won't work either. Don't own a cape, don't have a cave, a butler, a friend in the police department, gadgets, or a brain pickled in fury, or marinated in revenge. I might be a night person, but I'm hardly a Dark Knight.

So what was I? I was pissed, that's for sure. Pissed that I'd been tricked, my emotions played like a guitar; pissed that I'd been pushed to kill someone I didn't even know; pissed that I hadn't been there for someone I *did* know; pissed that I was so stupid I hadn't seen through it all; pissed that I still didn't have a damned clue what I was going to do.

Except see The Boy and, if I could, fucking kill him.

I stopped walking. I had about seven or eight blocks before I got to 17 Reasons. The night, as I said, was cool and misty. Traffic was light and people on the street seemed to be in a hurry to be somewhere else. They grabbed their elbows and trotted, they pulled up collars and darted. The stars were hidden behind a heavy curtain of overcast, the neon, fluorescent and incandescent signs were blurred of their vowels, the subtlety of their advertising becoming just BUY, EAT, USE, or SEX.

Slow, calming breath, chilly air stinging my nostrils, goose-bumping my arms. I tried to think in facts and not in PISSED (my own sign, way too brightly lit—meaning all too clear in my mind). It wasn't easy, but I tried my best. Tried to use my mind, and not be used by my guys. Think like Saul.

Not easy to do, as he had a few thousand years on me—and was a Hebe ("Let's not forget that, boychick"). But let's give it a shot: The Boy was other, different, a flip-side child, the shadow of a monster or a twisted god. He was a being of cryptic meaning and puzzling motivations. He was strange, as strange as anything sipping lymph and blood soup in the morgue or as anything half-seen, partially viewed in the fogs of the uncertain Sunset.

But if he was so powerful, so mighty, so great, so dangerous, so bizarrely muscled in magic, glimmer, or charm, then why didn't he get his hands dirty? He liked puppets, tricks, and mirrors to get other folks to do things. Me with Julian, Pogue with . . . whoever.

Maybe he was less great and powerful, not as strange and deadly, not quite as odd and mighty as I had thought? Maybe he was small and fragile, tiny and weak, puny and soft, needing his puppets, tricks, and mirrors because he couldn't do anything else?

Okay, I wasn't Clint, Oaks, Coburn, Bronson, Cleif, Fonda, Wayne, or Scott. No way could I be Gotham's protector—and I was beginning to realize that Saul had nothing to worry about, either. Me replacing him, I mean. So I had to find another way of looking at this whole thing.

And so the question: What would Pogue do?

* * *

Orders came in at 0600. We were to take Hill 1317. That's what the brass called it. We all had another name for it: The Boy. Last time anyone tried to take that lump of fucking rock, no one came back. What a way to start a fucking morning.

We'd been bivouacked since 2000 hours the night before. Just enough time for the guys to get some shut-eye and some chow. We'd spent the last eight hours playing hide and seek with a fucking great piece of heavy armor that took it personally that Beef had messed up its camo with an RPG, and everyone just wanted to close their eyes and forget about this stupid fucking war for a few hours. Spick was the only one who hadn't filled his belly with cold rations and crawled off for some sleep. He'd been the one who'd finally lured the armor into a ditch by the main highway, leaving it for the Air Force to finally ventilate, so he was high as a fucking kite. Naturally, I stuck him on watch. Use those damned wide-open eyes of his for some good.

Having to take the hill wasn't going to go over well with the Toughs, so I let them sit on their sorry asses as long as I could. Then I kicked the ones who'd pissed me off and just yelled at the other motherfuckers until they were all awake enough to hear what I was saying.

Tell ya, lucky I'd saved their fucking lives only a few days before, 'cause if I hadn't, I think they would have field-promoted Sergeant Frog on the spot with a bullet to my brain.

"What the fuck?!" said Beef, always a fucking master of the language, when I told him where we were going and what we were going to do. Even less articulate with the same message, Greasy just threw his kit across the clearing.

We broke camp and were all set to head out at 0700. But then Red snuck up behind me to report that he'd just found Spick fifty meters from camp, his throat slit ear to ear.

That's when I realized we'd have to wait to die another day. Orders were orders, but someone had killed one of mine, and I wasn't going to do anything until we caught the fucker and gave him a personal lesson in the horrors of war.

Pogue . . . was dead. Julian wasn't. Julian hadn't even existed. Pogue had. Julian had been a dream, a beautiful, sweet, wonderful dream. Pogue had been the bastard that other bastards called "bastard," and meant it. I'd loved Julian, more than I'd loved anything or anyone in my previous life or my current undead one. Pogue, I'd wanted dead. A lot.

But I'll tell you, straight and true—well, gay and true, or just true, or whatever—if Julian had been real, hadn't been just a lie The Boy had dreamed up to make me go nuts and take out Liam, I still wouldn't have wanted him with me right then.

I was walking, slowly, down 18th Street toward a building with a cryptic sign saying 17 Reasons, to walk up a flight of stairs and confront a being of unknown abilities, with puzzling motives. And I'd have done anything to have Pogue, the bastard's bastard, with me.

* * *

Only a few blocks left. The city had gotten busier the closer I got to the Mission. Still cool, almost cold, the night was still signs blurry by mist, pedestrians bundled and scurrying down the sidewalks, but now there was an aroma in the air—and not just of beans and roasting meat, tortillas and tequila.

The Mission might have been dirty (in parts), scary (in parts), creepy (in parts), but it was always lively, very much alive. Catching bites of salsa spilling out of dark bars, smelling roasting corn and that wormy booze, it made me feel weird. It was alluring, a Latin siren song to step off the street into a taqueria or into one of those musty dives for a plate of something spicy and a shot of something strong. Start over, put all this behind me. Just vanish. Not have to deal with The Boy, not have to go back to being the worst cop in the world.

A pair of brown eyes, perhaps. A set of strong lips. Hands on my body, my hands on his body. Simple. Direct. No confusion about what was right and what wasn't. No responsibility.

No, not anymore. That Valentino was gone, died either with Julian or with Pogue—which, I wasn't quite sure. But when I'd died . . . again . . . wasn't as important as the grave marker and the epitaph: SCREWUP NO MORE.

I had a job to do and, being scared or not, not knowing what to do or not, my knees banging together or not, I was going to do it.

Or so I thought, just before I got hit in the head.

* * *

Okay, you may say it: *Ouch!* Because that's exactly what it was like. Never been hit in the head with a fastball, never been punched in the forehead, never had an anvil fall on my head, but that's what I imagined it felt like.

One minute I was walking down 18th Street toward Mission, my purposeful stride back, my focus focused, my direction clear, my hopes up, my pride inflated (well, sort of), when I was smashed in the side of my head with what felt like a fastball, a fist, or a sideways-flying anvil. One minute walking up to the top of the world again, the next lying on my back on a sidewalk smelling of urine (used tequila) and vomit (used tortillas), my head reeling and swelling.

As quickly as I could, I crawled back up to my feet, bracing myself by leaning against a brick wall faintly bouncing from bass-heavy music playing behind it. Once my vision cleared and the spots stopped doing the backstroke, I looked right, then left, then right again, trying to see who or what had sucker punched me.

To the right was nothing but half a block and the busy streaks of nighttime cars on Mission Street. On the corner was a pair of dark-haired guys who looked more interested in scoring (or selling) dope than throwing shit at undead gay men.

To the left was a darkened street, only a few glowing windows showing where the apartment buildings began and the sidewalk ended. Illuminated, caught in some spilling light from one of those windows, was a couple out for a stroll: a Mediterranean-shaded woman with dark curls and a tall drink of water in a beard. Neither looked like the kind to bean-ball anyone, let alone me.

I looked to the right again, and my pair of guys were still on the corner, whatever suspicions I may have had falling away when I was still staring at the backs of their heads. If they had thrown something, they no doubt would have been looking to check on my damage, if for nothing else just to gloat and laugh.

So what the hell had happened?

Shaking my head again, still trying to clear it enough to think, I tried to scope the rest of the area, thinking that maybe some asshole, fuckhead, or dickwad had decided he didn't want my kind (vampire or fag, I didn't know yet, but, considering my mood, he'd be telling me that and a whole lot more if I got my damned hands on him) in his neighborhood.

But there was nothing—or at least nothing I could see. Just street, cars parked on it, windows hovering on either side of it, streetlights making pools at either end, the couple walking toward me, the two guys on the corner still being nothing but two guys on the corner. Nothing else. Zip.

As far as I could see, of course.

Just about the time I had given up and was about to head back toward 17 Reasons, it happened again: smack, *ouch,* and down.

Lying there, stars again, swelling again, really pissed again, I climbed back to my feet, determined to catch who was doing this and neatly, enthusiastically break him in half over my damned knee.

But first I had to see. It took a little longer this time but finally my eyes stopped spinning around in my skull and the light show faded back into just a thundering headache that I thought would split my head like an overripe cantaloupe—if whoever had been either slugging me or throwing shit at me didn't do it first.

Right, left, right. Two guys on the corner, still looking to score or sell; couple a bit closer but still too far away to have thrown something; two guys again, no sale, no buy.

What the fuck was going on?

Then I heard it. Very faint. Very, very faint. In fact, take your average faint and cut it in half, then half again. That's a little louder than how loud this sound was. Like a quarter of a mosquito. High-pitched, a whine that came and went, one ear then the other, like something very small with very fast wings was orbiting around my sore and swelling head.

I was about to think, and maybe even say, *"What the fuck is going on?"* again when the tiny little bean that was my brain rattled around in the coffee can that was my skull and happened to hit just the right point for a memory to come out, and with the memory, a thought.

The buzzing got louder, whining around my right ear. I ducked and wove, trying to put some distance between it and me. I didn't have a lot of time, but enough—I hoped—that I could get that bean to work again for a way to get me the fuck out of this.

Whine again, dodge again—but this time I was slow and the half of a quarter of a portion of a mosquito grazed my forehead. Even though it wasn't a complete impact, it hurt like you wouldn't fucking believe.

I ran. Instead of right or left or right again, I bolted across the street, lucky that the traffic had thinned. Once across, I twisted around, trying to catch a glimpse of what the hell was coming after me.

I was treated to a show. On the other side was a bit more light, some spillage from a watt-liberal apartment owner one floor above me. Illuminated by the glow was a dancing gnat, a tiny point of shimmering reflection. But it wasn't a mosquito, a gnat, or anything else with weird eyes or more than two legs.

Bean in coffee can, memory and thought. The memory was Saul, talking to me about a being that people thought could vanish or turn invisible but really couldn't. A critter that was very old, very mysterious, and ate years the way I drank blood, leaving its victims either older or just a pile of dust.

What followed was a personal introduction: The tiny winged thing headed right for me but just before it got to my sore head it stopped, slowed, and pulled back until it was about a dozen or so feet away from me.

Then it grew. Up from half of half of half it came, more stretching or unfolding or undulating than actually growing, like it was pulling itself up from out of some deep hole in the stuff of reality and not just gaining size.

He was handsome, I have to say that. Red-haired, fair-skinned, body tight and firm under a neat little Tommy Hilfiger outfit, all white and cream (shirt and pants), pale blue (piping and some periwinkle details). His face had some strength, more pretty than handsome, but not fluffy or icing like the Marys had been. A face and body to dance with, to kiss, to be seduced by.

I was in big trouble.

Valentino the vampire, meet Liam the faery.

Then Liam the faery spoke and I knew I was really, really in trouble.

"For The Boy!" he yelled, and came at me swinging.

XIX

I knew how he felt. Oh, boy, did I. Love of your life, murdered before your very eyes. The killer's neck right in front of you, sweet, sweet taste and feel of revenge only a squeeze away. Only one stipulation, a requirement to say just one thing.

"For The Boy!" Liam said, aiming a fist at my poor, wounded head again.

Either he was slowing down, which I doubted, or I was getting used to his pounding—full-size or miniature—and so knew what was going to happen if I didn't move and damned quick. So I did, back away from his blow.

"Wait!" I said, weaving to the left when his clenched fingers went for my head again.

"Stop!" I said, ducking to the right when he aimed another one for my noggin.

"Hold it!" I said, bobbing to the right when he fired yet one more bruiser at my dome.

"I didn't—" I said, twisting to the left when he tried to crush my skull, "—do anything!" I bent to the right when he punched straight between my ogling eyes.

Nothing. Zilch. Nada. Not a glimmer, a flash, a twinkle of anything but muscle-clenching fury, iron-jawed rage, furious vehemence, and quaking ferocity. No reason. No thought. No understanding, except for wanting me very, very dead.

I knew how he felt. Oh, boy, did I. All too well. I'd felt the same way myself, only a day or so ago. In fact, I would have done the very same thing to him, if I hadn't woken up on a rooftop in the bright rays of the sun, then heard that someone else made the same call, that same stipulation, a requirement.

The Very Bloody Marys

doi:10.1300/5329_19

Yeah, I knew exactly how he felt. He was going to try to kill me. In fact, there was a good chance he'd do it.

I was in trouble.

* * *

Reason was out. That much was clear. But, still, I tried again anyway. "Wait! Stop! Hold it! I didn't do anything!" But his Irish eyes stayed non-smiling and glassy, his face remained set in cruel stone. Punching toward my head, his hands remained tight, bony fists.

I wove, ducked, bobbed, twisted, and bent away from him, trying to keep enough distance between him and my more vulnerable bits. So far I'd succeeded; so far he hadn't smashed my melon into gray seeds and wet rinds, but I didn't know how long that'd last.

I knew what I was: vamp, bloodsucker, old fart without the wrinkles or the dentures, fast healer, sunlight hater, and all the rest of it. But Liam the faery? All I had to go on was a few tidbits of conversation between The Chef/Coroner (unreliable and shifty) and Saul the Wizard (reliable and crafty) and a lot of hollow hopes and total guesswork.

The only thing I really had going for me was the wonderfully reassuring notion that if Liam the faery had something really weird, totally nasty, and very supernatural, he would have used it already. Right? Right? Right?

Then he scored on me. Maybe I'd weaved, ducked, bobbed, twisted, and bent a tad too slowly, a bit lazily, or maybe his two (or was it three?) head shots had seriously scrambled my vampy, blood-sucky, old-farty dome.

Whatever the cause, the result was nasty and unpleasant, at least for me. One moment I was feeling that I might actually get out of this with some of my supposedly immortal hide intact, and the next this skin, bone, and tendon missile screamed out to pop me right upside the head.

If I really was the Man with No Name, the Dark Knight, or Sergeant Pogue, I'd have grinned right back at him, wiped the blood from my chin, and said something dark and manly, like "That the best you got?" "Enough kissing; let's fight," or "Try again. I didn't even feel that."

But I wasn't. I was Valentino, and even though I'd done a lot of growing up in the past few days, it hurt like a goddamn motherfucker. I said *"Ow!"* and danced backward, hoping he wasn't going to follow up with another shot.

As said, unpleasant for me, but for him it must have been Christmas, New Year's, his birthday (do faeries even *have* birthdays?), and Easter rolled into one, because his stone had cracked, his frozen face melted for just an instant of wonderful pleasure at rattling my brain in my skull.

Okay, that was it. No more Mister Nice Guy. Not that I'd been all that nice before, but I think you get what I mean.

Pogue had tried to teach me how to fight and I'd love to say that some of his screaming, spittle-flying, ass-chewing, browbeating lessons had stuck, but they hadn't. Nope. Not a one. Truth to tell, this defender of the lighter side of the dark world simply screamed (trying to make it sound ferocious but probably just sounding like a cat being stepped on) and came at him swinging wildly.

Luck. Sure, I'd heard of it. Never really encountered the good side of that coin. Bad side, plenty. Good side, not a helluva lot, but I guess that night, on that street, in that instant, I flipped my personal quarter high into the air, and it landed heads up.

Which is right where I hit him. It was a good hit, a solid hit, fist-to-skull impact, a very satisfying hit, if I do say so myself in a bit of ridiculous pride. The problem is that the instant my fist smashed into his melon, I knew I'd probably hurt my hand more than him.

Or maybe not, because while I danced around going "Ow! Ow! Ow!" and flexing my fingers to see if any of them were broken, he tripped backwards, smashing hard against a parked car.

Pogue's fighting might not have stuck, but some of that bastard had stayed around because I was sure I heard his roaring voice in my ears: "Move it, you fucking moron! Get in there and take out his fucking ass!"

Sir, yes, sir! Which was what I did. Curling my bruised hand up into a fist, I took two long, slow-motion steps toward his sprawled faery self, meaning to grab him by the collar, haul him to his feet, and inflict some kind of manly, testosterone-heavy beating that would make me feel really good and might have even made that old bastard Pogue smile a bit, for once.

But then I didn't. Yeah, I know: dumb. Very, very dumb. Spectacularly dumb. Incredibly dumb. Amazingly dumb. But that's me, right?

The fact is, I just couldn't do it. I didn't know Liam, didn't know where he was born (are faeries even *born?*), didn't know if he was a good faery or a bad faery, didn't know if he told a good joke, didn't know if he liked to take moonlight walks, didn't know if he kicked kittens, didn't know if he sang in the shower, didn't know if he ate babies.

But I did know one thing. I knew how he felt. He'd lost someone, maybe even a few hours ago. Someone warm, wonderful, and special. A dream. A person who'd meant everything to him. And, as far as he was concerned, I was the one who'd killed him.

That wasn't a crime. That wasn't worth beating him for. There had to be another way.

I knew something else. Something that made me swear ("Oh, fuck"), because just as my fist began to uncurl, Liam vanished, shrinking down to his tiny, winged self. A form that could move almost faster than I could see and that could probably pound me to pudding without me being able to do anything about it.

* * *

I ran. Boy, I seemed to be doing that a lot lately, eh? But I'll tell ya, when it comes to three mincing vampires or one majorly, severely, incredibly pissed-off faery, very often discretion—i.e., cowardice, if you want to be less formal—is better than getting your skull split open.

So . . . bye! I turned, and I ran, hoping that I'd knocked him around, maybe, possibly, enough that he'd be too dazed to do anything but buzz around under a streetlight for a few minutes, give me some time to put a large quantity of feet between his majorly, severely, incredibly pissed-off self and my sore and scared self.

No such luck. I didn't get farther than maybe a car's length away from where I'd left him before a damned hard missile traveling damned fast smacked me between the shoulder blades, sending me tumbling, sprawling, collapsing to the very, very hard sidewalk.

Okay, fight didn't work. Flight didn't work. What the hell was left?

"Listen up, you piece of vamping dog shit! You fucking spew of diarrheic filth! There will always be some other shit, some other badass, who is fucking meaner, fucking tougher than you. The trick, you scum on the bottom of my fucking shoe, is to use the one fucking muscle they aren't using. *Comprende?*"

Crawling back to my feet, I tried to scope him out, track his buzzing flight pattern to at least try to figure out the direction from where he'd come at me next.

So much for that plan, as well. I thought head shot again, thought my back again, thought maybe my chest, or maybe even (yes, you may shudder) my balls, but I didn't think of my legs.

The right, specifically. A highly accelerated gnat with the weight of a full-grown faery, however heavy that was (whatever it was, it sure wasn't light) smashed into my right thigh, taking me right down again. Crumple. Smack onto the cement. Ouch.

Luckily my brain was still working, even though my leg had been added to my list of very bruised, maybe even broken, body parts. When I hit and sprawled again, I also rolled a couple of times, leaving nothing but bare sidewalk where I'd first fallen.

Good move, that. Maybe my only one. But still, a good one. I knew what the weight of a full-grown faery was like when it hit my head, my back, and now my leg, but I now knew the sound a fully-grown faery made when it hit bare cement.

It was a good sound, for me. For him, I imagined—hoped—it was less so.

But it bought me a bit of time, time I spent getting up and pushing myself into another run. I really didn't think that had finished him, but I prayed to whatever gods vampires pray to that it would daze him enough to get me as far away as possible.

Maybe I was getting used to this, all this running and fighting, because even though my heart was smacking my ribs all to shit and I was breathing molten lead, my brain was actually working, a hurricane of thought and memory and plot and plan.

I was missing something. I ran it through my windstorm mind, trying to get something to stick just for a moment. What had The Chef said? What had Saul said? What had Pogue said? What the hell was I going to do?

Making themselves smaller? Check, as per the maybe bruises, maybe broken bones on my face, back, and leg. Immortal? I hoped not. Sucking years from humans? Possibly. I hoped that vamps were exempt.

There was something else. I knew it, or at least I knew that I was forgetting it. I tried to walk back in time, rewind the past few days to me standing in The Chef's kitchen, in Saul's kitchen, to remember what exactly they'd said about faeries.

I might have if I'd been able to keep running and so keep thinking, but just as I swear I felt the first bubbles of recollection come up from the big, black forgetting in the back of my churning and frenetic mind, I got slammed again. Bullet time. Fast traveling faery time.

Fuck! Damn! Shit! That hurt; right between my shoulder blades again. What was with this guy and the same spot? My face, then my back—again. This time I didn't go completely down. Instead, I spun, twisted, and danced with my own numb feet and managed, just managed, to stay on them—at least long enough to shoot out an arm and snag a sickly little urban tree for support.

Okay, I wasn't on my back on the ground, which I guess was an accomplishment. But as far as accomplishments went, it wasn't a major one, as the moment I got my balance back I heard, very clearly, distantly, and frighteningly, the buzzy, gnatty, beey, mosquitoey sound of another painful smack to the head, back, or leg.

I might have been able to duck the little so-and-so if I could see him, but the problem with not being a day person (aside from the pallor, of course) is that the world is usually pitch-fucking-dark, and the problem with pitch-fucking-dark is that you can't see a fucking thing. Especially not something half the size of something half the size of something barely visible in the middle of the brightest fucking day.

Liam the faery, though, could see very well, thank you (fucking much), as I found out when he broke his nice little pattern of beatings to hit me in the shoulder. I swear, I don't really know what being shot feels like but I also swear that Liam the faery smashing into my shoulder felt very much like it.

But I didn't go down; give me that much. On my feet, I waved my hands around, hoping that some part of my wildly flailing hands would return the smacking favor.

Heads again. Lucky again: I hit something, that's for sure. Something very small and very, very hard. Okay, it wasn't maybe the smartest stunt I'd ever pulled; in fact, I knew it wasn't, because the problem with hitting something very small yet very dense is that it's very much like being hit by something very small yet very dense.

Ouch. Man, oh man, I was getting sick of that. Really sick. But I was damned if I knew what to do about it. I doubted I'd get another shot at him, and even if I did there was a pretty good chance I'd look into his hypnotic eyes again and not be able to follow through.

Shit and damn and fuck.

The buzzy, gnatty, beey, mosquitoey sound was back. In fact, it sounded even more buzzy, gnatty, beey, mosquitoey than it had before. Great, oh great. Now he's *really* pissed off.

Come on, Chef. Come on, Saul. Come on, Pogue. One of you said something. But it wouldn't come for my frantic weaving, ducking, bobbing, twisting, and bending to avoid his buzzy, gnatty, beey, mosquitoey fury.

God, what would Pogue say if he could see his shit-for-brains, grease-stained, putrid, washed-up, no-account, scum-sucking, complete-and-total-asshole of a trainee getting his brains and back and leg and shoulder beaten to steak by a . . . faery?

What would he say if he could see me. See me?

See me see me see me see me see me see me see me see me see me see me see me see me see me. . . .

Thank you, sir! You are the best, sir! You are a prince among men, sir! I could kiss you on the lips, sir!

And you, Saul, my one friend in all the world, who happened to have said what had finally floated to the top of the stinking toilet bowl that was my oh-so-unworthy brain.

Faeries, I finally remembered, are vain. They can be trapped by their reflections, hypnotized by their own beauty reflected back at them.

Okay, I had something. A little something. A slim something.

But there was one problem—and it was a damned big one. Where in the world, where in hell, where on Earth, where in the Mission District of San Francisco in the middle of the night, was I going to be able to do anything with my slim little piece of precious information?

In other words, how was I going to find, and use, a mirror?

XX

Times like these (like this?), I really hated that my life (my undeath?) wasn't like it was in all those movies, books, plays, TV shows, comic books, etc.: Liam comes after me in his faery outfit, all small and fast and wingy, so I put on mine, all small and fast and batty. Liam won't listen to reason, so I just stare into his Irish eyes and tell him to calm down, quit, stop it, and he does. Liam bashes my brains in, fists flying, bits of my skull flying, and I just wait until he's done and put myself back together again, dust myself off, and take in a late movie. Maybe something with Nicolas Cage. Always thought he was hot.

But I couldn't bat it up, hypnotize, get smashed up, and put myself back together again. All I could do was what I had been doing, which was run around, shriek like a little girl, get pounded to a pulp, and hope hell below and heaven above (myths and illusions according to the few I knew who were in the know) that I could try to think of some way, any way, to avoid the pulp-pounding resulting in me dying, completely and totally.

The problem is I had only one real idea, and no way to pull it off. Mirrors, you see; I had to do it with mirrors. At night, in the Mission, while Liam was trying to expose my misfiring brain cells to the nighttime air.

Speaking of Liam and what he wanted to do to me, he did it to me again: a whine like half and half and half again of a mosquito, a crack to the side of my already bruised and already very sore head. I had been standing. After that I wasn't standing anymore.

Okay, no mirrors. But maybe this time he'd listen to reason:

"Wait! Stop! Don't! *Hold it!* I didn't kill anyone—hell, I wouldn't kill anyone. Well, it's not like I haven't killed anyone, just not anyone you know. I mean, I haven't killed anyone for a long, long time. Well, except for three bad vamps I locked on a rooftop, but I don't think you knew them. Well, I hope you didn't know them. Anyway, what-

The Very Bloody Marys

doi:10.1300/5329_20

ever it is you think I did, I didn't do it. Really! Honestly! For fuck's sake, quit hitting me!"

Of course he didn't listen. Of course he didn't stop. All he did while I was ranting and raving and pleading and sputtering was scream "For The Boy!" again and beeline–or half of a half of a half of a half of a mosquito–right into my chest, pushing me back, bruising me up, and making me crash into a parked car.

Spine painfully against an import, I ransacked my sore brain for another alternative. I might have thought of one if he hadn't swooped at my temple, making me duck down. Mister Forehead, meet Mister Side-View Mirror. Ouch, and then some.

Then it hit me. The mirror, I mean. Both insight and impact. As soon as the stars retired to the old stars' home and my vision returned, I grabbed hold of the side-view mirror and tried to wrench it off.

But that would have been too easy. That's the problem with foreign cars these days. Too fucking well made. I pulled, tugged, jerked, punched, slapped, and strained to try to get it away from the car. I twisted, twirled, spun, and forced to get the damned thing to bend back toward Liam. But that coin I'd previously mentioned refused to come up heads again, no matter how many times I flipped it.

It was only after the faery buzzed my brains again that I finally realized that there were other mirrors out there.

In hindsight (okay, that was a bad joke), I would have stopped and thought this all through, but I didn't. Instead, I bolted to the next car, and the next, and the next one after that. Only to discover that it wasn't just foreign cars that were well made, and even when they weren't, it was still the middle of the night, in the Mission, and it would have taken a miracle—or at least a lot of heads coming up from a lot of coin flips—for Liam to be able to see himself in a mirror only a few inches across.

This revelation descended on me after the fourth car, when I finally got one of the mirrors to come free and I waved it around, trying to catch the faery in silvery glass—and for my trouble getting slammed right in the solar plexus by 150 pounds of near-rifle-velocity supernatural, and very pissed-off, being.

It hurt. A lot. I wish I could say I was getting used to it.

* * *

Yeah, I wished that I was the vamp from the late show, from the stage, from *Tales of the Undead* #156, from *Dark Shadows,* and all the rest of that. But after Liam punched me in the gut and I found myself curled up once again on the sidewalk, I wished for one more thing: that I could be the vamp that Pogue had been. A mean-ass vamp, a hard-as-nails vamp, a vamp that would have broken Liam in half, a vamp that would have taken no shit, a vamp that would have saved the day.

A vamp that would have saved my fucking ass.

Buzz, buzz, buzz. So I rolled, but this time Liam the faery was smarter. No smack into the sidewalk this time. Damn. Instead, he pulled away at the last minute, the high-pitched whine of his change of direction ringing in my ears.

Yeah, Pogue. *The* Pogue. Pogue of brass balls and a steel jaw. Pogue of muscles on muscles. Pogue of the right thing at the right time.

Pogue that was dead. Yeah, that pissed me off; yeah, that made my fingers into fists; yeah, that made me want to kick some ass. But then I realized something else. Pogue was dead, and no matter how much I wanted, wished, and hoped, he wasn't coming back. But he'd done something while he was back among the living, or the undead, or whatever it was we were. He'd been my boss, which meant he'd been training me.

Not someone else. Me. There had to be a reason for that. Sure, the *Conseil* had made the ultimate decision, but Pogue had seen something that had made him come around to agree with them about it. He'd seen something in me.

He might not have said it, but he never gave up either. There was something in me. There was something in me.

Lying on the sidewalk, I had one thought in my head: *Fuck this.* Then I got up.

It felt really fucking good.

Okay: think. Not a lot of time. I couldn't—or wouldn't—outfight him, but there had to be another way. Mirrors were out. Even if I could get my mitts on one, there was no fucking way I could get Liam to stand still long enough to get hypnotized by his own reflection. There had to be another way.

Think, think, think. Reflection: Faeries like to look at themselves. They love looking at themselves. Why do they like looking at themselves? Because they are pretty. But if they knew they were pretty they wouldn't need to look at themselves. So why do they get lost in their own reflections?

Vanity. Insecurity. Do you need a mirror to be flattered? To have your vanity stroked?

Of course you don't.

"Liam!" I screamed, hoping that would make him pay attention, or at least slow down his buzzing, buzzing, buzzing in preparation for another dive-bombing attack on my already beaten and smacked-up body.

"Listen to me, Liam!" I yelled. "Pay attention! I have something very important to tell you!"

The buzzing, buzzing, buzzing slowed, but not by much. He wasn't exactly in a good frame of mind for an in-depth discussion about anything, unless it was how to decorate the lampposts with my guts. I didn't have a lot of time.

"Y-you're gorgeous! You're really, really pretty, Liam! The prettiest, most handsome faery I've ever seen. And, believe me, I've seen more than my fair share of them and I have to tell you that they don't even hold a candle to you. You're the best! You're incredible, amazing, wonderful, fantastic—" and I really wished I owned and carried a fucking thesaurus—"pretty, attractive, and all-around the most superb faery in all the world. You look up 'Wow!' in the dictionary and your picture's there—or it would be, but people keep stealing the dictionaries just for your picture. You're that great! You're so striking that people lose track of what they were about to say, you're so distract. . . . What was it I was going to say? You know, I can't remember! I get lost in your eyes, Liam! I'm trapped, mesmerized, by your beauty, your fantastical and oh-so-sexy self! If you don't mind me saying so, you're the kind of . . . being . . . someone could spend the rest of his life with, each and every second staring at your perfect arrangement of eyes, nose, lips, hair, and all the rest of your . . . your . . . your splendor. Yours is a magnificence that is completely . . . magnificent! You're the one, man! The one and only!"

I wasn't dead. I couldn't believe it. Dead, not me.

"You're it! You're absolutely, perfectly, wonderfully it! Beauty is you! Pretty is you! Liam, you are an ideal! Did I say that you are great? Did I? You know, you are so damned fantastically . . . wonderful. Did I say that as well? Listen to me, Liam, I'm so out of it, out of it because I am simply entranced by your overwhelming attractiveness!"

Then no more buzz, buzz, buzz. No more tiny, but really damned heavy faery. Instead, full-grown-and-right-there Liam. Liam of the (and I have to say I wasn't *that* far off with my overdone flattery) Irish beauty.

No time to believe my own bullshit, though. No time at all. His face was still firm and set, his eyes hooded and dark, his lips tight and pale, fists at his side, spine too straight. But those fists weren't flying, landing any punches or blows.

"Liam, oh, Liam. You are a prize, a treasure, a wonder, a true and honest beauty. You are a person worthy of being respected. You're handsome, yeah, you are, but not because of the way you look but because of all your bluster and thunder, all your insults and screams. You really do care, don't you? You don't want anyone to know that, that you have a heart under all that armor, hidden under the bullets and the uniform, but you do, and that's what makes you really, truly special. But you are. You are. People see it. Maybe it takes them some time, maybe even after you're gone, but they . . . I do see it. Thanks. Thanks for everything."

Liam looked puzzled. Not that I could blame him. Not after that. But even if he was confused, his face stayed firm and set, his eyes remained hooded and dark, his lips were still tight and pale, his fists continued to be at his side, and his spine—as before—too straight. His fists didn't fly, landing no punches or blows.

Yeah, I knew a bit of what he might be feeling, having lost a dream, having it killed before his eyes. Yeah, I knew his heartache, sympathizing way too much for his situation, his condition in all this. We were fucked-over brothers, kin under the skin, the league of the screwed over.

Still, I had things to do. So I hit him. It was a good punch, from way down low and full of clenched muscles and good trajectory. Pogue, I hoped, would have been proud of that punch.

Man, it hurt—me, for sure. One of those things you never see, or read about, is how much it hurts to really hit someone in the head. Believe me, if people knew, they would stop themselves from doing it.

But the pain in my hand was more than worth it. Satisfaction, sure, for getting a shot in, but also because it worked. It really did. Liam, shock flickering across his psychotically furious rage, collapsed—and on his way down, his Irish dome collided into the door of a car parked behind him. This was a very, very good thing, as I doubted I had it in me to toss another one of those damned things at his face. It hurt too damned much.

Call me cautious—or just overly sympathetic—but I pulled him away from the car, and also checked that he really, really was out like a light. He was breathing, which was good, or at least I hoped it was for a faery.

He was down. He was out. *Oh, man,* I breathed, deep and long, *thank fucking god.* I sat down next to him, one, to watch him, and two, because now that the adrenaline was pouring out of me, my legs were quaking and quivering too much to balance on them.

Sprawled, he didn't look like much. A handsome guy (like I said, I hadn't been lying all that much) on the sidewalk. I hoped that he'd either stay down for a good long time or when he woke up he'd return to his senses.

Breathe in, breathe out. Hands in front of my face, still shaking but not as much as they had been. I debated clenching them back into a fist but I'd done enough of that—and probably would have to again before the night was done. The right was really sore, and I distracted myself with the fantasy that it was broken.

Now what? I knew what I had to do—hell, what I *wanted* to do—but I just sat there, air going in and out of my lungs, one hand hurting and shaking, the other just shaking.

I felt different. How different, I didn't know yet. Maybe after this was all over. . . . But for now it wasn't, so I was in limbo.

I was about to start wondering what I was going to do about my faery problem (in other words, what to do about the wheezing and supine Liam) when I heard a familiar sound: an eight-cylinder, Detroit-special kind of noise, one that immediately conjured up the memory of a plush backseat, scuffed leather, and used springs, and the back of a black neck pocked with zits and curling stiff hairs.

I wanted to say "Where the hell were you?" but didn't because I was more than weirdly happy to see him. Getting up wasn't fun, as the adrenaline had left behind cramps and stiffness, but I did it anyway. Sure enough, double-parked was my ride, the cab's engine idling like a small earthquake.

I also wanted to say "Help me with this guy, will ya?" but didn't because I knew he would never get out of that cab and, as I've said before, having caught that one glimpse of his face (shudder), I really didn't want him to, even if it did mean me having to manhandle Liam from the sidewalk into the backseat.

Which is what I did. Ask me if that was fun, by the way. Go ahead, ask me. Well, I'll tell you anyway: Fun, it was not. But I managed to do it anyway. In some way, it worked out very well, because I'll bet you that dropping him a couple of times as well as banging his head on a car bumper helped keep him unconscious for a little bit longer.

Propping him up on that wide leather seat, making sure his head wasn't flopping too much, I slammed the door with a very firm sense of total relief. "Take him somewhere safe, will ya? I have work to do," I said, knowing that Mariah would keep him busy for as long as it took him to shake it off. Hard to continue to be dangerously furious when you're trapped in the backseat of a cab on the freeway.

Off they went, taillights fading into traffic in a few seconds, the pair of them vanishing into a sea of similar brights.

Yeah, work to do. The Boy to see, The Boy to kill.

XXI

For the Conseil*? For Ombre? For the nameless victims of the Bloody Marys? For Vanilla? For Green Tea? For Chocolate? For Liam? For Liam's illusionary love? For Saul? For humanity? For vampanity? For Julian, even though he didn't exist? For Pogue? For duty? For revenge? For justice?*

For me?

A number and a word. Meaning a location: "17 Reasons." A bad part of town, an ugly part of town. A thrift store on the outside, something more than bad, something ugly down deep on the inside.

I walked, feeling the night. Funny, how long I'd lived in it but rarely, if ever, really felt it. Like the air: invisible, always present, but then the wind comes and you realize how big and powerful it is.

I walked, feeling like I *was* the night. Funny, how long I'd *lived* but rarely, if ever, really felt like I was alive. Like the air: invisible, always present, but then the wind comes and you realize how big and powerful you can be.

Or, I should say, how much I hoped I could be.

A block, then less. The city flowed and rushed around me, humans and probably a lot of their flip sides: the others, the different, the shades, shadows, monsters, demons, and creatures that just looked like them. Going about their business, living their short or long lives. I crossed Mission, bathed in the stopped headlights of a few behind their wheels, their businesses high octane or simply regular.

Then I was there. A door, dog shit, *Fuck you*s, and hypodermic needles. Ugliness camouflaging something even uglier.

I went in.

* * *

He was illuminated. That hadn't changed. He was angelic. That hadn't changed either. In fact, nothing had changed. The Boy was

The Very Bloody Marys

doi:10.1300/5329_21

still The Boy: perfection and glowing, ideal and light. Standing at one end of the room, gleamingly beatific, simply looking at me.

"You failed," was all he said.

It. Was. Hard. To. Talk. Too illuminated. Too angelic. Too perfect. Too glowing. Too ideal. Too light. Too gleaming. Too beatific.

I wanted to say I was sorry. I wanted to whimper. I wanted to whine. I wanted to beg forgiveness. I wanted to cry.

Wanted to, yeah, but I didn't. I don't know where my refusal came from: From the *Conseil* giving me the job? From Ombre? From Julian's death? From Julian not existing? From Saul's caring? From standing up to The Chef? From surviving the rooftop? From killing Vanilla? From killing Green Tea? From killing Chocolate? From beating Liam? From Pogue? From Pogue getting killed? Lots of possibilities, maybe even more than seventeen reasons, but all that mattered was that I didn't.

"You failed," he said again, and as he did he became even more illuminated, more angelic, more perfect, more glowing, more ideal, more lit, more gleaming, more beatific. Growing, he gained an inch, then two, then three. Shadows danced on the walls, cast by his brightness. The air began to crackle, like lightning about to blast. Floating, his golden hair formed a faint halo around his head.

Gritting my teeth, tensing every muscle I could, I didn't again. No apologies, no whimpering, no whining, no regrets, no tears.

"Yeah," I managed to say; how, again, I had no idea. "About that—"

"You failed!" This time, no gold and silver, no choir or chorus, no bells or harps, no music or harmony from The Boy. This time it was blood and thunder, crashes and doom, pain and suffering, death and destruction. The Boy wasn't just illuminated; that had changed. Now he was burning, waves of heat rolling and churning off his bare shoulders, blistering and smoking the beams over his head, blistering the polished floor under his feet. Before innocence and concern, now his eyes were swollen blisters of hate and malice.

I took a step back, then two. I would have taken three but the door was behind me. I would have opened it and taken that third but . . . I didn't. I was on a roll.

"YOU FAILED!" God was mad. Jesus was pissed. Buddha was spitting. Allah was raging. You name a deity and he, she, it, or they were in that room with me and they were fucking *pissed.* The room shook and rattled, dust trickling down from the beams, rivers of it running down the walls. Cracks raced and met hunks of plaster. The floor buckled and warped, and the window behind him (which, as it was the last time, was showing a nighttime scene of the city beyond) exploded in a hailstorm of glittering daggers and spinning crystal knives.

Ducking down, I shielded my eyes, feeling a few of the tumbling fragments sting my bare arms.

This, and I know I'm stating the obvious here, was bad. Very, very bad. I don't know what I expected, but The Boy blasting, blistering, burning, and booming sure wasn't it. I guess I thought that after dealing with three pissy vamp queens on Vespas and one psychotically upset faery I could handle one "Boy," even if he was something other than he appeared.

I guess I simply hadn't realized exactly how "other" he was.

Okay, this was it. This was the time. For the *Conseil.* For Ombre. For the nameless victims of the Bloody Marys. For Vanilla. For Green Tea. For Chocolate. For Liam. For Liam's illusionary love. For Saul. For humanity. For vampanity. For Julian, even though he didn't exist. For Pogue. For duty. For revenge. For justice and, most of all, for me. I couldn't let some "Boy," no matter what he was, no matter what he could do, get away with this.

The problem was, I had no clue what I was going to do.

* * *

What he might have lacked in originality he definitely made up for in intensity. Repeating himself with even more volume, he went from simply toasting me and roasting the ceiling to a real fiery effigy, an outline silhouetted by roaring flames.

I had options, none of them good. I could take that third step and get the hell out of there, my forked vampire tail between my pimply ass cheeks; I could apologize, whimper, whine, beg for forgiveness, and cry my brains out; I could charge in with arms flailing and get burned to a curled-up little crisp (ouch!); I could flatter him into paralysis (hey, it worked once); I could trick him into coming up onto the roof (hey, it worked once); or I could simply stand there—which, with all those choices, was what I ended up doing.

I tried to think, tried to get hold of the part of me that had tricked the Bloody Marys onto that roof, had tricked Liam into standing still long enough for me to deck him. It was slippery, that little bit of me. Was it *there?* Nope. Was it *there?* Zilch. Was it *there?* No luck.

The Boy was an inferno, a bellowing, raging demon from a really bad part of a really bad place. His voice was the syllables of doom, his tones the clanging bells of Armageddon.

I couldn't think. I couldn't think of what I could do, what The Chef had said about The Boy, if he'd said anything; what Saul had said about The Boy, if he'd said anything; what Ombre had said about The Boy, if he'd said anything; or even what Pogue might have said, if he hadn't gotten his stupid ass killed.

I was terrified. I was quaking in my tennis shoes. My knees were knocking and my teeth were chattering but I was also so angry that I couldn't think of anything to do—except get roasted alive.

So, nothing to lose, I did the only thing I wanted to do. I screamed, as loud as I could, my voice cracking, squeaking, and snapping: *"Shut the fuck up!"*

And wouldn't you know? It worked.

* * *

But shutting up wasn't the only thing he did. Not that he was a chatterbox, you understand (at least not this time I was in the same room with him), but the instant I told him to shut up, he was about to speak, his bellowing mouth already beginning to form words. He just never completed the action.

But, like I said, that wasn't the only thing that didn't happen. No burning, no roasting, no charring. The flames still blurred his outline, but the inferno that had been surrounding him seemed to—screw that, it *did* ebb, did fade, did diminish.

I was onto something.

"Yeah, that's right, you heard me," I said, arms crossed, glaring, staring him down. Okay, it actually came out more like "Y-y-y-yeah, th-th-hat's r-r-right, y-y-you h-h-heard m-m-me." What if Elmer Fudd and Porky Pig had a baby? But give me some credit; it may not have come out as smooth as I wanted it to, but that it came out at all was worth *something*.

And he got even smaller, even dimmer, even cooler, even fainter: I was really onto something.

"I said shut the fuck up and I fucking mean it!" This time that's exactly how it came out, my own rumbling, my own cannon roar. Well, okay, maybe a rifle if I was lucky, but it was definitely not a quivering, quaking voice I was using. It felt good. Damned good.

"You goddamned piece of fucking shit! You piece of supernatural filth! You're not worth wiping off the bottom of my boots, you diseased maggot! You're nothing but a damned floater in my dimension, a turd in my fucking piece of reality! You make me *sick*!"

Part of me understood what was going on, part of me "got it" as I watched him reduce, shrink, fade, and chill. Monster to demon, demon to man, man to Boy. Flames to warmth, warmth to cool, cool to cold. Beauty to average, average to homely, homely to ugly. Tricky, that's what he was. That's the way he worked, getting other poor folks to do his dirty work. *Why* was clear: because he couldn't do anything else. Smoke and mirrors, tricks and magic, but down deep he was nothing but a cold, ugly child.

Part of me didn't care. It felt too damned good.

"I should just kick your fucking ass," I said, taking steps—but forward, not back. One, two, three, and with each, The Boy shrank more and more and more. "I should break you in fucking two."

At four steps, he was only a crooked figure, bent and sniveling, eyes cowering at me from under a twisted shoulder.

"But you're not even fucking worth it, you miserable sack of fucking shit!"

I stopped, close enough to see that his perfection was wrinkled and scaly, what was once beauty now just cracking scabs and seeping ulcers, the broad avenues of bulging veins.

"But I've got a message for you. You listening, scum? You comprehending me, garbage? Do I have your complete and undivided attention, you pile of excrement? Do you hear me*? Do you fucking hear me?!*"

Hairs tumbled from the top of his head, once-golden locks now greasy and stringy strands sticking to his quivering knees on the way down to the floor, a floor sprinkled with the golden jewels of leaking piss. Tumbled as he nodded, nodding as he tried to tell me he did hear, did understand.

"I CAN'T HEAR YOU!" I let it out, all of it: the frustration, the anger, the fury, the rage that had been capped and bottled down there in my chest. It felt good. It felt marvelous.

"Y-y-y-y-y-y-y-y-e-e-e-e-e-e-s-s-s-s-s-s . . ." he slurred and hissed, the voice of a beaten mouse, a whipped cockroach, a pathetic ant. I could barely hear him.

"Then get this: comprehend it, fucking understand it, pay attention. I catch you here again, so help me, I am going to unscrew your neck and piss down your goddamn throat. I will rip your damned arms off and beat you to fucking death with them. I will shove my boot so far up your fucking ass that you're going to be coughing up the dog shit I stepped on the rest of your fucking days."

One more step, and he was nothing but a suggestion in the air, a ghostly form curled up tight, a quivering fetus hovering a foot or so above the floor.

"Do you know why?" I said, my voice no longer as frustrated, no longer as angry, no longer as furious, no longer raging. That had passed and inside I was just like my voice: calm, relaxed, certain, and centered. It felt better than marvelous. It felt right.

I don't know whether he heard me, as he was now but a microscopic miniature, a shimmering comma surrounded by a slowly pulsing, unearthly glow.

I didn't care. I had to say it anyway. "Because I am Valentino, and I'm an officer in *Le Conseil Carmin, Le Corps Policier Contre,* and San Francisco is my responsibility. It's my duty to protect and to serve it. *This. Is. My. Town.* Understand?"

Still didn't know if he heard me or not, because the comma that had been The Boy was no longer lingering, no longer glowing or hovering, no longer bright or ugly, wrinkled or perfect, hot or cold.

I was alone. He was gone.

XXII

Walking, but not just walking. My strides weren't long, hesitant, or really all that strong. During my stroll back from the Mission, leaving behind my reasons (all seventeen and more), I wasn't angry, frightened, or even all that purposeful, though I did have a purpose in mind. Nah, the walking I was doing was just right. Simply perfect. The best kind of walking there is or ever could be.

But, still, even as I walked my ideal walk, I wasn't all that happy.

I missed him.

I didn't think I could, after all that had happened, but I did.

Things had changed, that much was clear, but the city was still the city, the night was still the night, the world was still the world.

Halfway down the block I saw a shop that wasn't there, a sign saying MEL'S SHOES hovering fuzzy and indistinct, superimposed over the modern facade of a too-clean, too-plastic, too-fluorescent, chain video store. Mel had obviously cared a lot about his little repair business, pounding just enough tiny nails into soles, sticking tough threads through tongues, buffing, polishing, so that when he finally passed away enough of himself had remained behind to give SHOES an afterlife of its own. That was my city.

At the corner, I noticed I was being watched. During the day it was a knot, a gnarl in a tough old urban tree, a dark-barked thing of twisted branches cracking the dark sky and knuckled roots cracking the gray cement of the sidewalk. But when I caught sight of that one knot, that special gnarl, it blinked in response. It was a playful wink, a joke shared between two things—that tree and I—that lived between sunset and sunrise. That was my night.

Crossing the street, I saw a dog walking his man. Hey, who am I to judge? The guy was pale and slight, a Caucasian whippet—that kind of breed. Pulling at his leash, he darted and pranced as far as the

The Very Bloody Marys

doi:10.1300/5329_22

strand could let him. On the other end, his master was a great shaggy beast, happy to be out with his pet, enjoying their time together. No one else might have seen them that way, but I did because I walked the same flipped, twisted, reversed existence they did. That was my world.

Not far now, just a few blocks. Blood, bath, and bed—in that order. Tomorrow night. . . . I didn't know what I was going to do tomorrow night. But the rest of tonight was a sip of cheap red, steam and dirt going down the drain, and crawling between the sheets.

But then, between two painted ladies (Victorian homes to you folks who don't know the city) a section of black, a patch of deeper ink than the rest of the night. Oh, and a voice: Maurice Chevalier, Louis Jordan, Claude Rains, or, Jean Reno. "Monsieur Valentino?"

"Yeah?"

"Any news as to the current situation, *s'il vous plait*?"

"You could say that, yes."

"The rogue vamps? The Very Bloody Marys?"

"Burned up."

"Ah. The unusual manifestation I mentioned previously?"

"Gone as well. He . . . it . . . won't be coming back."

"What of Monsieur Pogue?"

"He's dead."

"Unfortunate. He was a good man."

"He was."

There was a moment, then. Something between the worlds, between the hard night and the inky black between those two buildings. Then he said, "Very well then. Keep up the good work."

And I was alone.

* * *

Yeah, I shouldn't have. But I did. I missed him. Almost home, my thoughts drifted around, swirling like the water that could soon be descending down my drain.

At my door, that swirling bubbled spontaneously. Blood, bath, and, most important, the bed, reminded me of dust at the foot of it, of someone crumbling away in my hands.

The time he'd held my hand, looked straight into my eyes and said those all-important three little words. The sun had been in my eyes and the hillside we were lying on had been thick with wildflowers, but neither of them were what had brought tears to my eyes. I remember his hands, strong yet delicate, the nails looking like mother-of-pearl, the faint veins the periwinkle of fine china.

The time we'd slept in, sycophantic breathing after a matching set of orgasms. Paris outside the window, bread and wine on a tiny wooden table. He'd put his head on my chest, mumbling "thump, thump, thump" to my heartbeat until he breathed a little slower and faded off into a gentle little sleep.

The time we'd walked on the beach, holding hands, he whistling one tune after another, the game being whether I could name them. "Ode to Joy," "Marriage of Figaro," "Beethoven's Fifth"; the prize for a successful guess a kiss on the cheek. I remember it being the most important game in all the world, the prizes the greatest of my life.

I put my key in my lock and turned. Blood, bath, and bed. Life as usual.

Julian never existed. There was nothing there to miss.

* * *

Hot pennies. I read that somewhere. The way that blood tastes: like hot pennies. Copper and salt. Sipping the very last of my supply, this time with a nice hit of vodka in a kind of celebration, I glanced around my very empty kitchen. Not much there; no need when you don't have to cook.

It was okay. It really was. The bad guys were gone, duty had been discharged. Another day at the office.

I knew what I was going to do, after my bath and some sleep. There really wasn't any choice, and what was really weird, as well as kind of nice, was that it was okay with me. Back to work. Another day at the office.

It wouldn't be the same though.

The time Mister Horror decided to haunt Fisherman's Wharf. Pogue and I, slipping between the tourists and the low-paid locals, looking for a phantom in a cape and thick stage makeup. The host of a local TV show took his cancellation very hard, his character even more so. Basically dead if not performing in front of people, his ghostly persona took to frightening the Bermuda shorts and I'M WITH STUPID T-shirt crowd. I'd found him first, a rare and special thing, pointing out the overacting specter. Pogue had just turned to me, a tilt of the head that was the closest thing to a smile and said: "Good job, son."

The time that Colma, around here known as the Land of the Dead for its surfeit of graveyards, hit critical mass. One too many burials and the soil rejected them all in one ectoplasmic hurl, a blue-white wave of crackling, deathly energy surging down the streets, cresting over the buildings, a torrent of once-dead-now-not splashing over the city. The daytime folks out for a nighttime stroll couldn't see it, of course, but we and the rest of the twilight people could. It was terrifying. But not as much as having to swim upstream through it back to Colma, where we dug up the corpse that had tipped the scale. Covered in grime, reeking of formaldehyde, bits of the dead covering us, we sat on the edge of the grave as the wave rolled back. He turned to me then, said with laughter mixed with his usual grumbling tones: "Ain't this a bitch of a job?"

The time we'd been standing, just standing, on the corner of some street or other. I think we were between jobs, or maybe between long, hard bouts of training. But whatever. Whatever. We were just standing on a street corner and the silence came down, stood between us. Heavy and dark and oppressive. I was about to break, it being so bad, but then he did something I'd never seen before: he turned to me, cleared his throat, and said, "Dull fucking night, eh?"

The time the nicotine craving got pissed at the patch, the gum, at Addicts Anonymous and all the rest of our insulting acts of self-control. Smoky and coughing, it blew into town, breathing cancer and emphysema into anyone who crossed its billowing, silvery path. For weapons, all we had were a pair of Chinese prayer fans—which we'd hoped to use to blow it into another world. The battle was fought in Union Square, the craving blown away by Pogue's skill and determination. Me? I missed, sending a bad mime tumbling ass over teakettle down the street. After, when things were quiet and calm, he'd said "Nice shooting, Tex," but between the words was the message that it was okay, because I'd done my best.

The time Ambrose Bierce came back, Bitter Bierce having become Sad Bierce after having seen the corruption and ineptitude of the other side, or at least the corner he'd seen since falling off that horse in Mexico. We sat with him for an hour at least, while his spirit sobbed. Finally he'd cried it all out and he faded away completely, making a trip to (hopefully) somewhere better than the afterlife. Unexpectedly, right in the middle of the next night's training, Pogue asked, and clearly meant: "You okay?"

He'd been a bastard, an asshole, a prick, a fuckhead, a dickwad, and so much worse. I'd hated him. Hated him a lot. Nothing was good enough for him and he always took time out of his busy schedule to tell me I could do better.

I stripped, walked into the shower, and let the water pound my face and chest numb, wash away the grit and grime of the last few days.

But it couldn't wash Pogue out of my mind.

* * *

Lather, rinse, repeat. Lather, rinse, repeat. Lather, rinse, repeat.

Then rinse and dry. But halfway between the bathroom and the bedroom I had to stop. There, at the foot of the bed was where Julian had faded, crumbled, dust to dust.

Julian. Perfect and handsome Julian. Ideal and wonderful Julian. The man of my dreams. The man who'd been created just for me. Only for me. Woven carefully through my mind and memory, slipped in there so well I didn't know he was a trick until it was almost too late.

Julian, a reflection of everything I'd ever wanted in my life. Woven throughout my years, months, days, hours, minutes, and seconds, he'd been crafted by The Boy to die and leave the greatest, deepest, most painful possible wound. Born to die. Died so that I'd kill.

But I didn't miss him. I missed an asshole, a prick, a fuckhead, a dickwad, and so much worse.

When it had all come down, with the Marys, with Liam, with The Boy, Julian hadn't been there, hadn't given me anything. Pogue, though, had. He'd been there, yelling and screaming at me from a corner of my mind, giving me the strength to deal with it all.

Deal with it all. Yeah, that made sense.

Into bed. But once again sleep only hovered nearby, not yet dropping down onto my eyelids, filling my head with dreams. I missed Pogue.

Tomorrow I'd deal with it. Tomorrow I'd try to figure it all out. Business as usual as a *Le Corps Policier Contre* in *Le Conseil Carmin*. A visit with Saul, for sure, to see my pal and let him know that Julian was a manipulative figment, and that all was once again right with the world. A trip to the morgue, absolutely, for a nice little sit-down with The Chef to see if he had anything to do with the Very Bloody Marys. Then check out the city, see if anything else had cropped up, any new or creepy thing that had crawled into my night, my city, my world.

Yeah, business as usual. But better than usual because I knew, for the first time, that I really was good enough to deal with it all. I had it. It might not be polished, complete, and fully assembled, but at least I knew it was there.

Thanks to Pogue. He'd believed in me—so, naturally, I had to as well. After all, he wasn't someone you disagreed with.

No sleep, not yet. My eyes were wide open. Ladies and gentlemen, Valentino might be a bit slow (okay, he is *very* slow), but eventually he does figure things out. It might take him a few years, months, days, hours, or minutes, but the answer will come in time.

Julian was the man of my dreams, everything I'd ever wanted in a boyfriend, and my life.

Pogue was an asshole, a prick, a fuckhead, a dickwad, but he'd also taught me what I needed to know. He'd never given up on me, even though there were plenty of times when he really should have.

I guess it's not what you want, but what you need.

* * *

But that wasn't it. Not all of it. Not yet.

Toss, turn. Turn, toss. Repeat. There was something else bothering me, something else preying on my mind.

Yeah, Pogue was what I'd needed. The kind of person who would kick my ass to the curb, who'd slap me around, force me to be what I could be, not what I'd settle for.

But there was another question not answered. It had to do with bed, with sheets. It had to do with Pogue. It had to do with what I needed, not what I wanted. It also had to do with Julian, but in a twisted, mixed-up way.

A tug, a tickle, a tweak of sleep. I could feel my body begin to relax and fade into rest. But then it went away and was replaced by a bolt of revelation, an exclamation point of realization.

Yessiree, Valentino *is* slow (hideously slow, if you must know), but he will figure things out if you give him enough time. It might take him a while but the answer will come eventually.

Not that it made me rest any easier.

See, I'd been in bed before, when I'd thought about how Pogue had died, trying to take on the Bloody Marys single-handedly. How he'd been tricked, just like I had been. He'd had the person of his dreams, his dream lover, his perfect person, die.

I didn't know who that fake person had been. But deep down, somewhere around my heart, my little vampy soul, I couldn't help but wonder or foolishly hope for one single answer about who that person might have been.

It wouldn't change anything; not really. Whatever the answer was, it couldn't take away what had happened to me. I'd started to really grow up, to become more than what I'd been before. It was good, it was wonderful, it was marvelous, and who knew where it could lead to? Maybe it would all become even better, more wonderful, more marvelous. It was the start of a trip. (Okay, after two hundred years; but, hey, it's where you go, not where you begin, right? Cut me some slack.)

Still, it would have been nice to know who Pogue had seen and who he'd lost. Not necessary, just nice to know that maybe, just maybe, he'd needed me as well.

Epilogue

Momma always said I'd never amount to anything. But seeing that that was two hundred-something years ago, I figure I've got some time to prove her wrong.

The Very Bloody Marys

doi:10.1300/5329_23

ABOUT THE AUTHOR

M. Christian is the author of the critically acclaimed and best-selling collections *Dirty Words, Speaking Parts, The Bachelor Machine,* and *Filthy.* He is the editor of twenty anthologies including *Amazons, Confessions,* and *Garden of Perverse* (all with Sage Vivant), and *Blood Lust* (with Todd Gregory). His short fiction has appeared in over 200 publications including *Best American Erotica, Best Gay Erotica, Best Lesbian Erotica, Best Transgendered Erotica, Best Fetish Erotica, Best Bondage Erotica* and . . . well, you get the idea. His first novel, *Running Dry,* is still available from Alyson Books. For more information see www.mchristian.com.

Dear Customer:

Please fill out & return this form to receive special deals & publishing opportunities for you! These include:

- availability of new books in your local bookstore or online
- one-time prepublication discounts
- free or heavily discounted related titles
- free samples of related Haworth Press periodicals
- publishing opportunities in our periodicals or Book Division

❑ OK! Please keep me on your regular mailing list and/or e-mailing list for new announcements!

Name ____________________

Address ____________________

STAPLE OR TAPE YOUR BUSINESS CARD HERE!

____

*E-mail address ____________________

*Your e-mail address will never be rented, shared, exchanged, sold, or divested. You may "opt-out" at any time. May we use your e-mail address for confirmations and other types of information? ❑ Yes ❑ No

Special needs:

Describe below any special information you would like:

- Forthcoming professional/textbooks
- New popular books
- Publishing opportunities in academic periodicals
- Free samples of periodicals in my area(s)

Special needs/Special areas of interest:

____

____

____

____

Please contact me as soon as possible. I have a special requirement/project:

____

____

____

____

The Haworth Press Inc.

PLEASE COMPLETE THE FORM ABOVE AND MAIL TO:
Donna Barnes, Marketing Dept., The Haworth Press, Inc.
10 Alice Street, Binghamton, NY 13904–1580 USA
Tel: 1–800–429–6784 • Outside US/Canada Tel: (607) 722–5857
Fax: 1–800–895–0582 • Outside US/Canada Fax: (607) 771–0012
E-mail: orders@HaworthPress.com

GBIC07

Visit our Web site: www.HaworthPress.com